Likes Me, Likes Me Not

Shore Thing

Two for the Road

Three fantastic stories in one big book!

Look for these

titles:

1 It's a Twin Thing
2 How to Flunk Your First Date
3 The Sleepover Secret
4 One Twin Too Many
5 To Snoop or Not to Snoop?
6 My Sister the Supermodel
7 Two's a Crowd
8 Let's Party!
9 Calling All Boys
10 Winner Take All
11 PS Wish You Were Here
12 The Cool Club
13 War of the Wardrobes
14 Bye-Bye Boyfriend
15 It's Snow Problem
16 Likes Me, Likes Me Not
17 Shore Thing
18 Two for the Road
19 Surprise, Surprise!
20 Sealed with a Kiss
21 Now You See Him, Now You Don't
22 April Fools' Rules!
23 Island Girls
24 Surf, Sand, and Secrets
25 Closer Than Ever
26 The Perfect Gift
27 The Facts About Flirting
28 The Dream Date Debate
29 Love-Set-Match
30 Making a Splash

mary-kateandashley

TWO of a kind

Likes Me, Likes Me Not
by Megan Stine

Shore Thing
by Judy Katschke

Two for the Road
by Nancy Butcher

from the series created by
Robert Griffard & Howard Adler

HarperCollins*Entertainment*
An Imprint of HarperCollins*Publishers*

A PARACHUTE PRESS BOOK

A PARACHUTE PRESS BOOK
Parachute Publishing, L.L.C.
156 Fifth Avenue
Suite 325
NEW YORK
NY 10010

First published in the USA by HarperEntertainment 2001
Likes Me, Likes Me Not first published in Great Britain by
HarperCollins*Entertainment* 2003
Shore Thing first published in Great Britain by HarperCollins*Entertainment* 2003
Two for the Road first published in Great Britain by HarperCollins*Entertainment* 2003
First published in this three-in-one edition by HarperCollins*Entertainment* 2004
HarperCollins*Entertainment* is an imprint of HarperCollins*Publishers* Ltd,
77-85 Fulham Palace Road, Hammersmith, London W6 8JB

TWO OF A KIND characters, names and all related indicia are trademarks of
Warner Bros.™ & © 2000.
TWO OF A KIND books created and produced by
Parachute Publishing, LCC, in cooperation with Dualstar Publications,
a divison of Dualstar Entertainment Group, Inc.

Cover photograph courtesy of Dualstar Entertainment Group, Inc. © 2001

The HarperCollins children's website address is
www.harpercollinschildrensbooks.co.uk

1

The authors assert the moral right to be idenfitied
as the authors of these works.

ISBN 0 00 718443 3

Printed and bound in Great Britain by Clays Ltd, St Ives plc

Conditions of Sale
This book is sold subject to the condition
that it shall not, by way of trade or otherwise,
be lent, re-sold, hired out or otherwise circulated
without the publisher's written consent in any form
of binding or cover other than that in which it is
published and without a similar condition
including this condition being imposed
on the subsequent purchaser.

mary-kateandashley

TWO of a kind

Likes Me, Likes Me Not

by Megan Stine

HarperCollins*Entertainment*
An Imprint of HarperCollins*Publishers*

A PARACHUTE PRESS BOOK

CHAPTER ONE

"You're kidding!" Mary-Kate Burke said to her sister, Ashley. "This place? We're supposed to have our Spring Fling dance in here?"

"Not just the Spring Fling dance," Samantha Kramer chimed in. "They think we're going to be spending all our free time here! Welcome to the new Student Union for White Oak Academy and Harrington."

"But it's just a warehouse!" Mary-Kate complained. "It's dark, it's grungy, it's smelly, and . . . and . . . I think I saw a mouse!"

"A mouse? Yuk! Where!" Dana Woletsky screeched.

"It went under there," Mary-Kate said, pointing to a pile of old mattresses in the corner.

Two of a Kind

Ashley gazed around at the dusty warehouse. She didn't see the mouse. But her sister was right – it was dark and grungy. And smelly.

Well, at least it's big, Ashley thought.

And the reason it was dark was because so much stuff was piled in front of the windows. The place was filled to the brim with old chairs and mattresses, boxes, out-of-date textbooks, broken brooms, and rusty old gardening equipment.

Once it's cleaned out, Ashley realised, *it's going to be a nice big space. With a little paint, some new furniture, lights, and a sound system, it could be a great Student Union.*

The warehouse was on the property of White Oak Academy – the New Hampshire boarding school that Ashley and Mary-Kate attended. Right next door was the Harrington School for Boys. The new Student U was going to be used by the First and Second Forms in both schools.

In other words, it was a dream come true as far as Ashley was concerned. The guys and the girls were going to be able to hang out together all the time – not just on the few days when they had the same classes.

Ashley was the head of the girls' committee in charge of fixing up the old building.

"Trust me," she said. "When I get done with it, this place is going to look fabulous!"

"Well, you're the boss," Samantha said. "Where do we start?"

"Just grab some stuff and start hauling it out," Ashley said. "Mr Frangianella will be here pretty soon to show us which stuff is trash and which is treasure."

"You mean we're supposed to touch that mess?" Dana Woletsky asked. "I've just had my nails done." She wrinkled up her nose and made a face.

Trust Dana to start complaining right away, Ashley thought. Dana was snooty and usually acted like she owned the whole school. She obviously thought she was the queen of the First Form.

"If you want to be on the committee, you've got to work," Ashley said.

"Fine," Dana said, inching towards a pile of boxes. "But what about the mouse?"

"A mouse? Cool. Where?" a boy's voice called out.

Ashley whirled round. A group of guys from Harrington were standing in the open doorway. They were going to help clean up the Student U, too.

Two of a Kind

"Where's the mouse?" Grant Marino repeated.

Ashley glanced at her sister and saw Mary-Kate blush. Mary-Kate used to have a real crush on Grant. "It ran under there." Mary-Kate pointed to the mattresses again.

"Forget the mouse," Ross Lambert said. "Let's start hauling this junk out of here."

Grant and Marty Silver moved towards the pile of stuff. "I'll be with you guys in a moment," Ross continued. "Just as soon as I have a talk with Ashley."

Ross wants to talk to me? Ashley thought. *Maybe he wants to ask me to the Spring Fling dance!*

Her heart skipped a beat.

Ross was the first guy Ashley had had a crush on when she came to White Oak. He had big brown eyes, sandy brown hair, and dimples. She was always a sucker for dimples.

Ashley knew Ross liked her, too. Sometimes they went out for a pizza or to a film. She even went to her first big dance with him. Ashley thought of Ross as her sort-of boyfriend.

Ashley pushed her long blonde hair out of her eyes and smiled at him. "What's up?" she asked, trying to sound casual.

"We're supposed to talk about the Student U," Ross explained. "I'm the chairman of the boys' committee."

Likes Me, Likes Me Not

Oh. Ashley's heart sank for an instant. *He only wants to talk about the Student U,* she thought. *Not about the dance. Maybe he hasn't thought about it yet.*

But then she realised that if he was chairman of the boys' committee, they'd be working together full time for the next two weeks!

"Let's check this place out," Ross said, marching through the crowded warehouse. He headed towards some smaller rooms at the back. Ashley followed him.

"This is just a cupboard," Ross said. He opened a door and closed it again.

"We can store decorations for the dances in there," Ashley said.

"Yeah, or build a shelf and use it for all the video games," Ross suggested.

Then he ducked into the back room. It was small and private. "This will be great for a games room," Ross said.

"Or a cosy little sitting room," Ashley suggested. "Can't you just picture it? Sofas, low tables, stuffed chairs. Like a coffee bar, but without the espresso machine. And maybe we could put one of the TVs in here."

Ross frowned. "Whatever," he said as he slid past her, back into the main room.

Two of a Kind

Hey, it was just an idea! Ashley thought, following him.

Ross pushed past the pile of mattresses. Ashley kept her arms held tightly at her sides. She was on mouse alert.

At the other end of the building, they found another small room. Boxes were piled up in front of a door leading outside.

Ross glanced at her. "How about a games room here?" he suggested, raising his eyebrows.

Maybe, Ashley thought. "Or a kitchenette," she said. "We could put a microwave in here, and the vending machines. That way the food won't clutter up the big room."

"Well, where are we going to put the video games?" Ross asked. "You don't want them in the back, you don't want them up here. . . "

"Hey, we'll find a place," Ashley assured him. "I was just brainstorming, okay?"

"That's the right word for it," Dana Woletsky commented loudly from the other room. "Ashley's brain is always in a storm!"

Dana's best friend Kristin Lindquist laughed.

Ross laughed, too. "Besides," he went on, "I don't know if we've got the money for a microwave. Not after we buy two VCRs and about a zillion video games."

Likes Me, Likes Me Not

Ashley frowned and thought about their budget. Ross was right – they couldn't buy everything they wanted. The two schools were going to supply all the major stuff – new furniture, vending machines, two TVs and a portable ping-pong table. But the student committees had a small budget. Ashley and Ross were supposed to decide how to spend it.

"Two VCRs?" Ashley argued. "Why do we need two? I thought we'd use our budget to get a sound system, strobe lights, and a mirrored disco ball for the Spring Fling."

"Oh, man, no way," Ross shot back. He shook his head. "Strobe lights are cool, but you can only use them at dances about twice a year. But if we get two VCRs, we can watch two different movies at the same time all year round." He paused. "On the other hand. . ."

Ross marched back into the main room and looked around. "You might have a point," he said, nodding. "Strobe lights might look really cool in here with the walls painted black."

"Black?" Ashley's voice rose. "Are you kidding?"

"Okay, red and black," Ross compromised.

Ashley gulped. "Uh, I was seeing this room in softer colours," she argued. "Like maybe peach and pastel sea-foam green."

"Ick." Ross made a face. "Peach is a wussy color."

"Look," Ashley said. "I know that the Student U is for White Oak and Harrington. But we're probably going to be using it more than you guys, since it's on White Oak property. And we're having the Lock-In here – the same night as the dance. So I think the girls should have more say about what colours we paint the walls. It's only fair."

"What's a Lock-In?" Ross asked.

"It's so cool!" Dana said, dropping everything and rushing over to butt in on the conversation. "It's an all-night sleepover, just for the First- and Second-Form girls! We get to bring our pillows and sleeping bags, and they're going to lock us in here..."

"With the mouse," Grant Marino interrupted. He shot Mary-Kate a secret smile, but Ashley saw it.

Wow, Ashley thought. *He's flirting with Mary-Kate! I'll bet he likes her.*

"Don't interrupt," Dana said. "Anyway, we get to stay up all Saturday night watching videos, playing games, and eating junk food..."

"And then at, like, six in the morning on Sunday, we go back to our dorms to sleep," Ashley jumped back in.

"Cool," Max Dorfman said. "Maybe we'll come over and raid the place."

Likes Me, Likes Me Not

"Not a bad idea," Samantha encouraged him.

"So, don't you see?" Ashley insisted. "I mean, about the colour of the paint?"

Ross shrugged. "We can argue about that later," he said. "First we've got to get this place cleared out."

He picked up a stack of folding chairs and headed for the door. Ashley grabbed a mattress and started dragging it. It was pretty heavy.

"Okay," she called after him. "But I have an idea."

Ross put the chairs down on the lawn outside. Then he came back to give Ashley a hand. He lifted one end of the mattress.

"What?" he asked.

"We should have a fund-raising do," Ashley suggested. "That way, maybe we'll have enough money for the strobe lights and the VCR *and* the video games. We can get everything."

"That's the brightest thing you've said all day," Ross said. He gave her a half-smile. Half – because only one of his two dimples showed.

"Great!" Ashley said. "We'll have a cake sale!"

"Cake sale? You wouldn't want to eat the brownies I'd bake, believe me," Ross joked. "How about a pizza sale?"

"No." Ashley shook her head. "We had a pizza sale for the choir last month, and we only made fifty dollars. How about if we offer to walk dogs for all the teachers who live here?"

"Not enough teachers have dogs," Ross said in a grouchy tone. "Look – do whatever you want. Just let me know, and I'll make sure my guys show up."

He yanked the mattress away from her and threw it on the rubbish heap. Then he glanced at his watch. "I've got to go," he said. "I've got an essay to write for history. See you later."

Wait! Ashley thought. *Don't go away angry!*

But it was too late. Ross was already striding towards the shuttle bus that would take him back to Harrington.

I really blew it, she thought. *That whole conversation went wrong. I'd like to start all over again!*

She watched Ross run across the green. But at the last minute, just before he hopped on the bus, he turned round and waved at her. And smiled.

Ashley's heart skipped a beat.

Maybe he still likes me after all, Ashley thought. *And if he does, maybe we'll be going together to the Spring Fling!*

CHAPTER TWO

"Where should we sit?" Mary-Kate said. She gazed round the dining hall with her lunch tray in her hands.

"All the tables are full," Ashley answered. "Except that one."

She nodded towards the only table with empty chairs. It was the one where Dana Woletsky and her friends were sitting.

Mary-Kate shrugged. "I think we don't have a choice." She hurried over and plopped her tray down – at the other end of the table from where Dana was sitting. After working all morning, clearing out the warehouse, she and Mary-Kate were both starving.

Two of a Kind

"So tell me everything," Mary-Kate said after she'd taken a few bites. "You and Ross spent a lot of time together in those small back rooms. What's up between you two?"

Ashley chewed her French bread before answering. Then she leant close to her sister.

"I like working with him," she said softly. "But he was being a pain. He didn't like any of my ideas."

"Like what?" Mary-Kate asked.

"Like my plan to get a sound system for the Student U!" Ashley complained. "He wants a second VCR instead. Can you believe that? How does he think we're supposed to have the Spring Fling dance without music?"

"I don't know," Mary-Kate said.

Ashley shrugged. "Anyway, he was really hard to work with," she said.

"Wow," Mary-Kate said. "I wonder why."

Dana Woletsky stood up at the other end of the table and looked right at Ashley. "If you can't get along with Ross," she said, "did you ever think maybe you're the problem? I mean, he's the sweetest guy in the whole world. At least he's always been extremely sweet to me."

"Hey," Mary-Kate blurted out. "This is a private conversation."

Likes Me, Likes Me Not

"I'm just trying to give you some much-needed advice, Ashley," Dana said. "All I'm saying is that you're much too bossy. Anyone would find it hard to work with you."

Bossy? Ashley thought. *Look who's calling who bossy.*

Dana picked up her tray and walked away. Fiona and Kristin trailed after her.

Ashley stared at them.

"I'm not too bossy, am I?" Ashley asked when they were gone.

"Define too bossy," Mary-Kate joked.

"Thanks a lot." Ashley rolled her eyes.

"No, really – you're good at organising things," Mary-Kate said. "That's why the Head picked you to be in charge of the Student U committee – right?"

The Head was their nickname for Mrs Pritchard. She was the headmistress at White Oak Academy.

"Right," Ashley agreed.

"Well, maybe Ross is good at organising things, too," Mary-Kate said logically. "So both of you want to run the show, and you end up getting on each other's nerves. You know – it's like too many cooks in the kitchen or something."

"I don't know what to think," Ashley said as they left the dining hall. "I only know I like Ross – and I want him to like me back!"

Two of a Kind

The twins strolled across the lawn, back towards their house, Porter House. It was a beautiful, cool, spring day in New Hampshire. Crocuses poked up through the grass.

"Hey! Ashley! Wait!" a voice called.

Ashley stopped and saw Phoebe Cahill running towards them. Phoebe was Ashley's roommate. She was wearing a pair of bright paisley bell-bottom jeans and a cute little bright orange top. Vintage, of course. Most of Phoebe's clothes were from another decade.

"Hey, Phoebe," Ashley called. "Let me ask you something. I'm not too bossy, am I?"

"What do you mean by too bossy?" Phoebe asked.

"Ha ha!" Mary-Kate teased. "I told you so."

"Stop it!" Ashley blushed. "Anyway, Mary-Kate already made that joke."

"Okay – you're not too bossy," Phoebe said. "Is that what you want to hear?"

"No, I want the truth," Ashley said.

"Well, the truth is, I'm bored!" Phoebe said, changing the subject. "What are we going to do today?"

"How about a trip to the shopping centre?" Mary-Kate suggested.

Likes Me, Likes Me Not

"Too late," Phoebe said. "We've just missed the bus."

"I know!" Ashley's face lit up. "How about if we rearrange the furniture in our room? Mary-Kate, you can help. We'll move our bunk beds to the window, so we can look outside while we're lying in bed. Then we'll push our desks to where the chests of drawers are. And put one chest of drawers on each side of the door. Your posters can go on the cupboard door, Phoebe. And the wastebaskets can go beside the beds. What do you think?"

Mary-Kate and Phoebe both burst out laughing.

"You? Bossy?" Phoebe teased. "No way. Just tell me where you want me to put my toothbrush!"

Ashley frowned. "Hey, that's not fair! I was just trying to think of something to do, since neither of you could decide."

"Okay." Phoebe smiled. "Anyway, moving the furniture sounds like a plan. It'll be fun."

"Easy for you to say," Mary-Kate joked. "You haven't been hauling junk out of the warehouse all morning!"

"Look at it this way," Ashley told her sister. "At least you're already dressed for it. You don't have to change into old clothes!"

"Fine," Mary-Kate said as they climbed the stairs towards their rooms. "But I still want to stop in my room and ask Campbell..."

She stared into her dorm room and gasped. Ashley peeked her head in, too.

The room looked different. It took Ashley a moment to figure out why. All of Campbell Smith's stuff was gone. Her posters... her clothes... her sports trophies... her bedspread... her stuffed animals...

All gone.

And Campbell was gone, too. Someone brand new was sitting on her bed instead!

"Hi," the girl said, smiling at Mary-Kate. "I'm your new roommate."

CHAPTER THREE

"New roommate?" Mary-Kate gulped. "What happened to Campbell?"

"She and I had to swap rooms," the girl said. "I'm Ginger. Ginger Halliday. I hope you don't mind."

Mind? Mary-Kate thought. *Uh... yeah. I mind. I mind a lot! I like Campbell.*

"Uh, I just didn't know they did that at White Oak," Mary-Kate stammered. "I mean, change roommates in the middle of the year."

Mary-Kate glanced at her sister and Phoebe, who were still there. Ashley looked just as shocked as Mary-Kate felt.

"It was sort of sudden," Ginger said. "Campbell

just moved out fifteen minutes ago."

"So is Campbell gone for good?" Ashley asked.

"Only for a few weeks – probably," Ginger said. She turned her head away and coughed. Then she brushed her bright red fringe out of her eyes. "I have lots of allergies," she went on. "And I've been ill a lot this year. My doctors think maybe I'm allergic to something in my dorm – or maybe to my roommate! Wouldn't that be funny?"

"Well, you'll definitely be allergic to Mary-Kate by the time you're done," Ashley joked. "She gets under *my* skin, anyway."

"Ha ha," Mary-Kate said weakly.

But secretly she thought: *This isn't funny!*

She didn't want a new roommate. She wanted Campbell back! Campbell was a lot like Mary-Kate – good at sports and a straight talker. The two of them had become really good friends.

"So you're moving in here?" Phoebe asked. "And Campbell moved into your room?"

Ginger nodded. "I was living in Phipps," she said. Phipps was the house next door to Porter House. "Campbell's my friend. When she heard I was ill, she offered to help out."

"What do you mean it's only for a few weeks?" Mary-Kate asked.

"Well, my doctor wants to try this for a while,"

Likes Me, Likes Me Not

Ginger said. "If my allergies clear up, then maybe he's right. Maybe I *am* allergic to my roommate! Or to her hand lotion or something. I don't know. We'll see."

Mary-Kate gulped and glanced at Ashley again. They both knew what that meant. If Ginger's allergies disappeared, then maybe she'd have to stay in Mary-Kate's room. Then Campbell would never come back.

"Wow," Mary-Kate said. "This happened so... so fast."

She tried to smile at Ginger.

It's not her fault, Mary-Kate thought, trying to be nice to the new girl.

"My doctor only decided last night," Ginger said.

"Oh." Mary-Kate couldn't think of anything else to say.

"Uh, look," Ashley said. "Maybe you guys want to get to know each other. Why don't you just stay here, Mary-Kate? Phoebe and I will go and move our furniture ourselves."

"Yes, boss-woman," Phoebe joked, bowing to Ashley.

Mary-Kate laughed. "Thanks," she said. "I'll see you later."

Ashley and Phoebe wandered down the hall to their room.

"I put my clothes in the cupboard," Ginger went on. "I had to hang a piece of plastic between your clothes and mine – just in case. Hope you don't mind."

"In case what?" Mary-Kate asked. "I have fleas?"

Ginger sort of shrugged and smiled. "I don't know. My doctor told me to do it."

She hopped off her bed – Campbell's bed – and grabbed a tissue to blow her nose. Then she stuck an inhaler in her mouth and breathed in the medication.

Mary-Kate checked her out quickly while her back was turned.

Ginger had very pale skin and was so thin she was almost bony. Freckles dotted her face and arms. She was wearing a pair of baggy blue jeans and a rust-coloured sweatshirt, with the sleeves pushed up.

"Who was your roommate?" Mary-Kate asked.

"In Phipps? Oh, Jamie Randolph," Ginger answered.

Mary-Kate waited for Ginger to go on, but she didn't.

"So are you two close? I mean, are you sorry you had to move here?" Mary-Kate asked.

Likes Me, Likes Me Not

"She's okay," Ginger said.

She's not much of a conversationalist, Mary-Kate thought.

She tried again. "Where are you from? Ashley and I grew up in Chicago. I think we're the only girls at White Oak from Chicago, if you can believe that. I'm a total Chicago Cubs fan."

"I'm from outside Boston," Ginger said. "Hey – whose biology class are you in?"

"Mr Barber's," Mary-Kate said. "Why?"

"Is Grant Marino in that class?" Ginger asked.

"Uh, yeah," Mary-Kate answered slowly. She wondered why Ginger was asking about Grant.

Ginger's eyes twinkled. "Sooo?" Ginger asked, leaning forward as if she expected Mary-Kate to spill her heart out. "Do you still like him, or what?"

"Oh, man," Mary-Kate said. "Don't tell me that old rumour is still going around! That's last year's news."

Mary-Kate winced, remembering what had happened. Mary-Kate had liked Grant – until Ashley wrote a story for the school newspaper's gossip column all about Mary-Kate's crush! Grant found out about it. After that, Mary-Kate could barely bring herself to look at him.

Until today, in the warehouse. *He's still cute,* she thought. She could hardly keep her eyes off him.

But was that any of Ginger's business?

"I just wondered if you liked him," Ginger asked again. "I mean, do you think he's good-looking? Would you go out with him if he asked you?"

Wow, Mary-Kate thought. *She doesn't let up! I wonder if she's asking me because she likes Grant herself?*

"Grant's okay," Mary-Kate said, changing the subject quickly. "Excuse me. I've got to go and floss my teeth."

She grabbed some dental floss and hurried out of her room.

This is ridiculous! Mary-Kate thought. I shouldn't have to floss just to get away from my roommate!

But as she went into the bathroom, she thought about Ginger's question.

Did she still like Grant – or didn't she?

And what about the big question: did he like her?

CHAPTER FOUR

"Ashley! I made it! I made the team!" Mary-Kate called, running across the school yard the next day.

Ashley whirled round. "What team?"

"The White Oak/Harrington Co-ed All-Stars Baseball team!" Mary-Kate blurted out fast. She shot her fist into the air, in a cheer. "We're going to play Danville Day School in a few weeks."

Ashley smiled and gave her sister a hug. "Way to go," she said. "But you're the super-jock. You always make the A-teams."

Yeah, Mary-Kate thought. *I do. So why am I so super-excited?*

She knew the answer in a heartbeat. In fact, she knew it the minute she had walked into the gym that morning and saw the names on the list of players.

Grant was going to be on the All-Stars team, too!

"It's just going to be such a blast," Mary-Kate said. "We start practising as a team next week."

"Cool," Ashley said. "But you're still going to help out with the Student U, aren't you?"

"Oh, I can't wait to haul more dirty mattresses," Mary-Kate joked. "Just pile 'em on."

"Listen, I'm going over there now," Ashley said. "We still have a few boxes to move, and some old pipes to haul out. And we've got to sweep the floor. Some of the guys are meeting us. Can you come?"

"Why not?" Mary-Kate said. "I can't think of a better way to avoid homework – or Ginger."

Ashley shot her sister a glance. "You don't like her?" Ashley asked.

"I suppose she's okay," Mary-Kate said. "I mean, she's nice enough – but she's definitely not Campbell. And she keeps asking me if I like Grant. It's really annoying!"

"Well, do you?" Ashley said.

"Don't you start, too!" Mary-Kate complained.

"I was just wondering," Ashley said. "Because there he is!" She nodded towards the warehouse.

Mary-Kate's head snapped round. There, in the

distance, she saw the guys from the Harrington committee: Ross, Grant, Marty Silver, David Friel, and Elliot Smith.

Her face lit up.

"So you do still like him!" Ashley said.

"Yes. But don't tell anyone," Mary-Kate whispered. "I don't want it all over the school, like last time!"

"Okay," Ashley agreed.

The girls started walking a little faster. When they reached the warehouse, the guys just stared at them.

Mary-Kate and Ashley stared back.

"What are you waiting for?" Ashley asked. "Let's go in."

"Who has the key?" Ross asked.

"Oh! Sorry," Ashley said. She reached into her pocket, pulled out the key, and unlocked the warehouse door.

Mary-Kate hung back, waiting to see what Grant would do. He shot her a smile. "You coming in?" he said. "Or are you afraid your sister is going to lock us all in here together?"

I wish! Mary-Kate thought.

"Whoa!" Elliot hooted. "Grant wants to go to the girls' Lock-In!"

"Don't forget to bring your nightie!" David teased him.

Grant smacked David on the arm and body-slammed Elliot. The other guys just laughed.

"So what are we here for?" Elliot asked as they stepped inside.

Mary-Kate looked around. The big warehouse was still dirty, but it was almost empty. They had practically finished cleaning it out yesterday.

"The boxes in the back room go into the skip outside," Ashley said, giving out orders.

"We'll get those," David said, motioning two guys to come with him.

"And those pipes," Ashley said. "They go out. And we've got to sweep."

"I'll sweep," Mary-Kate offered, quickly grabbing a broom. It sounded easier than hauling old cast-iron pipes.

"Thanks," Ashley said. "Ross and I should talk about the fund-raiser anyway."

Ross rolled his eyes, but he followed Ashley outside. The two of them sat under a tree, talking.

"You need some help?" Grant asked Mary-Kate.

"What – you mean I should give you half the broom?" she joked.

"I suppose that wouldn't work," he said, sort of shrugging.

Likes Me, Likes Me Not

He hopped up onto a wide windowsill and sat dangling his legs.

Mary-Kate kept sweeping. Marty and Elliot marched through the room with the few remaining boxes.

"You look like you're dancing with that thing," Marty teased her.

"Ahhh!" Elliot laughed. "Mary-Kate's date for the Spring Fling! A broom!"

"Very funny," Mary-Kate snapped, but they were already outside.

"Hey – ignore them," Grant said. "I'll bet you'll have a better date than that stupid broom."

"You think so?" Mary-Kate asked.

Grant nodded and shot her a shy smile.

I think he's flirting with me! Mary-Kate thought. Her heart started pounding a mile a minute.

"I don't know," she said. "I mean, the broom asked me first."

Grant laughed. "The broom's too tall for you," he said. "You need someone more your size."

Wow! Mary-Kate realized. *He* is *flirting!*

Was he trying to ask her for a date?

"Hey, did you see we're both on the All-Stars team?" he said.

"Yeah." She nodded.

"Well, I was thinking that maybe we could—" he started to say.

But Ross interrupted.

"Grant, man! Get a move on and haul those pipes!" Ross yelled, poking his head back into the warehouse.

"Okay, okay," Grant grumbled.

He hopped off the window and picked up the pipes with a groan. A minute later, the other guys joined him.

Bummer! Mary-Kate thought. *Why did Ross have to butt in right then? He almost asked me out. At least I think he was going to.*

"You kids about done?" Mr Frangianella stepped into the building. "I'm supposed to be watching you, but I've got some bushes that need trimming."

"Okay. Two secs," Mary-Kate said.

Quickly she finished sweeping, then hurried outside. Mr Frangianella took the key back from Ashley and locked the building up. The Harrington guys wandered off to get the shuttle bus to their school.

"Won't it be nice when the Student U is done?" Ashley said. "I mean, the guys won't always have to rush away. They can hang around here all weekend!"

"I know," Mary-Kate said dreamily.

She stared at Grant, watching him leave. His hair looked cute, even from the back!

"Hi," a voice behind Mary-Kate said. "What's up?"

Mary-Kate turned. Ginger had come up behind them.

"Hi," Mary-Kate said. "Not much. Just working on the new Student U."

"With Grant Marino?" Ginger said, grinning widely.

Mary-Kate gave Ginger a blank stare. What was she doing? Trying to dig up some more gossip?

"Yeah, he was there. And lots of other guys," Mary-Kate said.

"So does that mean you like him?" Ginger asked eagerly.

Give me a break! Mary-Kate thought. *Can't she think of anything else to talk about?*

"No way," Mary-Kate insisted.

Ginger shrugged. "Okay. Just asking," she said. "I've got to go." She turned and walked away.

"What's that about?" Ashley asked when Ginger was gone.

"She won't stop asking me about Grant," Mary-Kate confessed. "She's driving me nuts."

"I can see that," Ashley observed. "Your face is all red! But why don't you just tell her the truth?"

"I was totally embarrassed in front of Grant once before!" Mary-Kate complained. "It's not going to happen again."

Ashley winced. Mary-Kate knew what her sister was thinking. The rumours last time were all Ashley's fault.

"Well, I'm not saying a word this time," Ashley promised.

"Good," Mary-Kate said. "Me, neither."

Not until I know for sure if I stand a chance with Grant!

CHAPTER FIVE

"Don't look now," Ashley whispered to her sister. "But here he comes."

"Who?" Mary-Kate whirled round.

"Grant!" *And here comes Ross, too!* Ashley added silently. She felt her heart start to skip a beat.

It was another beautiful Saturday, a week later. They were holding a car wash to raise money for the new Student U. Ashley and Mary-Kate and several other girls had been washing cars all morning – and waiting for the guys to show up.

"Shhh!" Mary-Kate said. "I don't even think I like him any more. He's been ignoring me at baseball practice all week."

"Really?" Ashley's eyes opened wide. "Last Saturday he acted like he was nuts about you."

"I know," Mary-Kate replied. "It's making me crazy. Does he like me – or doesn't he?"

Ashley shrugged. "Who knows?," she said. "But if you care, you have soapsuds in your hair."

Both girls pretended to get busy with the buckets, soap, and towels. Out of the corner of her eye, Ashley watched Ross and Grant walking towards them.

"Hi," Mary-Kate said when Grant was near.

"Hi," he answered flatly. "Your hair's full of soap."

"So I've heard," Mary-Kate said. She reached back and scooped off a handful of suds. "Want some?" She held it out like whipped cream.

"No thanks," Grant said, turning away. He picked up a towel and started drying one of the washed cars.

Mary-Kate's right! Ashley thought. *He's changed completely from last week. Now he's barely speaking to her.*

She saw Mary-Kate's face fall.

I know how you feel, Ashley thought. Ross wasn't paying much attention to her, either.

Ross picked up the hose and started fooling around with it. He pretended he was going to squirt Dana Woletsky.

"If you get me wet, I swear I'll make you pay!" Dana teased Ross.

"Yeah? How much?" he taunted her.

"I'll think about it," Dana warned him, flashing her best smile.

"Ross, we've got to talk," Ashley said, interrupting them.

"What's up?" he asked.

"Well," Ashley said, "we still haven't decided how to spend the money for the Student U. And we've got to buy the paint. They're going to start painting tomorrow."

Ross shrugged and tossed the hose to the ground. "Whatever you want," he said.

"Really?" Ashley's eyes lit up. "You mean you're okay with painting the walls peach and green?"

"Whoa!" Ross said. "I didn't say peach. I'm thinking compromise. How about one black wall at least? And you can paint the other three that sea-foam colour, or whatever you call it."

"Now we're getting somewhere!" Ashley said, beaming.

"Oh, come on," Dana said, butting in. "Black and sea-foam green? That's yucky."

"Yeah," Elliot called. "You know – the colours of rotting flesh."

Two of a Kind

Ross, Grant, Elliot, and Dana all laughed.

"I think one black wall could look really cool with three sea-foam walls," Ashley insisted.

Dana muttered something under her breath, but Ashley didn't hear what it was.

Ross laughed again.

Why doesn't she just go away? Ashley thought.

"About the money," Ashley went on, trying to get back to the main topic. "Maybe we should go somewhere and talk about it – in private."

Ashley shot a glance at Dana, hoping she'd get the message.

"What's to talk about?" Ross asked.

"The disco lights, for one," Ashley started to say. "Everyone wants them. So I was thinking. . . "

"Okay, okay," Ross said, interrupting. "If you really want the disco lights, that's cool with me. I mean, I don't want half the female population of White Oak angry with me for ruining the dance or something."

"Really?" Ashley's face lit up again.

"Oooh, you've made her soooo happy," Dana sniped in a mocking tone.

A moment later, a teacher from Harrington pulled up in his white Toyota. "Can you wash this right away?" he called out.

"Of course!" Ashley said. She handed Ross a bucket of soapy water. "Here," she said. "You wash the front. I'll scrub the tyres."

Ashley walked around to the far side of the car with a big sponge and another bucket. She bent down to clean the hubcaps.

"Honestly, Ross," she called. "You won't be sorry about the disco lights. And besides – I've been thinking about how we could get the extra VCR that you wanted. If we make enough money . . ."

But before Ashley could finish her sentence, a whole bucket of soapy water flew over the car.

It landed right on her head, drenching her.

"Hey!" Ashley cried, jumping up.

Too late. She was a drippy, soaking mess. Her clothes stuck to her, and her hair hung like strings, plastered to her face.

Ross burst out laughing.

"What was that for?" Ashley snapped at him.

But then she saw that Ross wasn't holding the bucket.

Dana was!

Dana smiled. "Oops," she said. "I didn't see you over there. Sorry. You're so small."

"Very funny," Ashley said, shivering.

It was a warm day for April in New Hampshire.

But not that warm. Not warm enough to stay outside in sopping wet clothes.

"L-l-listen," she said to Ross, her teeth chattering. "I'm going to g-g-go and change. Maybe we can talk about this at lunch."

"Okay," Ross said with a shrug.

Ashley hurried back to her dorm and changed as quickly as she could. Then she ran back across the yard, to the car wash. But as she neared the spot, her heart sank. Most of the guys had left.

"Where did Ross go?" Ashley asked Mary-Kate.

"He went to eat lunch," Mary-Kate answered. "And I hate to tell you who went with him. Dana!"

Oh, no! Ashley thought.

Dana is trying to ruin things between me and Ross! If she keeps this up, he'll never go to the dance with me. Never.

CHAPTER SIX

"Campbell! Hi!" Mary-Kate called across the dining hall that night.

Mary-Kate had just come out of the dinner queue with her tray. Mrs Pritchard was on her way in. She gave Mary-Kate a frown.

"Mary-Kate, please try to wait until your friend is within earshot," the Head said. "That way you won't have to scream at her."

"Sorry, Mrs Pritchard," Mary-Kate said.

But she couldn't wait to talk to her old roommate. Mary-Kate had hardly seen her since she moved.

"Campbell!" she called again, softer this time.

Campbell waved and pointed to a table. Mary-Kate made her way through the dining hall and sat down. Four other girls from Phipps were already sitting there.

"Hi, stranger!" Mary-Kate said. "I miss you! How's it going in your new dorm?"

"It's okay," Campbell said. "I miss you, too. There's no one I can toss a softball around with."

Mary-Kate beamed.

"Ginger's roommate is funny, though," Campbell went on. "She cracks me up."

"Jamie Randolph? Really? How come?" Mary-Kate asked. She felt a little jealous.

"Oh, she's so clumsy," Campbell said. "I tossed her an apple last night, and she dropped it. But she was hilarious. She started talking in a weird voice as if she was a sports announcer: 'Jamie bobbles the apple for the tenth error of the inning.'"

"Doesn't sound that funny," Mary-Kate said.

"You had to be there," Campbell explained.

"Yeah," Wendy Linden chimed in from the other end of the table. "It was a riot. You should have been there."

I wish I had been, Mary-Kate thought.

She really missed Campbell. Hanging out with Ginger was not much fun.

"Hey – who has a date for the Spring Fling?" Wendy asked.

"I do," one of the girls from Phipps said. "Believe it or not, I'm going with Elliot!"

"You're kidding!" Wendy said. "He asked you?"

The girl nodded.

"Well, I'm going with Danny Strohmeyer," Wendy said.

"Cool," the other girl said.

"But you don't have to have a date – right?" Campbell asked.

"Of course not," Wendy said. "You can just go in a group. Lots of people don't have dates yet, anyway."

Mary-Kate was quiet. She didn't want to talk about this in front of everyone.

"The Lock-In is going to be amazing," Mary-Kate said, hoping to change the subject. "All the films, pizza, and popcorn we can eat!"

"I wish they'd lock the guys in with us!" a girl said from the far end of the table.

Everyone laughed, and most of the girls agreed.

Campbell leant closer to Mary-Kate and lowered her voice. "What about you and Ashley?" Campbell asked. "Are you two going with anyone?"

Mary-Kate shook her head.

But I'm still hoping! she thought.

"Well, I mean, who do you want to go with?" Campbell asked.

Mary-Kate sighed. There was really only one guy she liked right now. And if he didn't like her... what was the point?

"I can't think of anyone," Mary-Kate lied. "How about you?"

"Me? Nah. I'd rather go alone, I guess," Campbell said. "But I mean, would you go with Grant if he asked you?"

I can't tell her the truth, Mary-Kate thought. *I can't tell her I like him. Because if Grant doesn't ask me out — I'll look like a loser!*

"No," Mary Kate lied again. "No, I don't think I'd go with Grant. Unless maybe —"

"Campbell!" Wendy interrupted them. "We've got to get going. French class is in two minutes."

"Coming," Campbell said. She shoved a last piece of cake into her mouth. "See you, MK. Let's watch a ball game on TV some night." She hurried out after Wendy.

Mary-Kate was going to explain that Grant hadn't exactly been friendly lately. But Campbell was already gone.

Mary-Kate sighed. Why was everyone so interested in Grant all of a sudden? *I know Campbell isn't interested in him*, she thought.

I wonder if she's asking for Ginger?

CHAPTER SEVEN

"Mary-Kate! You're late!" Coach Fisher called.

"Sorry," Mary-Kate called back as she hurried toward the field for All-Stars practice. "Mrs Bloomberg kept me after my English lesson."

She grabbed her mitt and ran to take her position in the outfield. Her heart was pounding by the time she got there.

"No, no," Coach Fisher called. "I want you on second base today."

Second base? But that was Grant's position!

Mary-Kate saw Grant's head whip round. He glared at her for half a second.

Oh, great! she thought. *Now he thinks I'm trying to take his spot on the team. He'll hate me for ever.*

Two of a Kind

Grant's head drooped down as he started running towards the outfield.

Her stomach twisted into a knot.

This is no fun, she thought. She used to love baseball. And being on the All-Stars team with Grant was supposed to be the best!

But it was turning out all wrong.

"Shape up, Grant!" the coach called. "We're just trying this out for today. I want the best person for each position. The goal is to win, right?"

"Right," Grant answered weakly from the outfield.

"Come on, Mary-Kate!" Danny yelled, clapping his hands.

For the next hour and a half, Mary-Kate tried to concentrate on baseball. It was hard, though. All she could think about was Grant.

He's right behind me, she thought. *Planning to hate me for the rest of his life.*

When it was Mary-Kate's turn to bat, she couldn't stay focused. She hit a pop fly and was out after only one pitch.

She glanced at Grant for sympathy, but he looked away.

Coach Fisher kept them at practice till 7 o'clock. By then, Mary-Kate was starving. She had to run to get to the dining hall before it closed. She was the only person in there. Everyone else had already eaten – and most of the food was gone.

"Just give me some salad," Mary-Kate said to the woman in the cafeteria.

"Oh, come on, honey," the woman said. "You've got to eat more than that. How about some lasagne?"

For the first time in a month, Mary-Kate felt a twinge of homesickness. The way the cafeteria woman had called her "honey" reminded her of home. Her dad always called her "honey" when he knew she was upset about something.

"Okay," Mary-Kate said. She took the lasagna, sat down, and picked at her food. At least it was still slightly warm.

Shape up, Mary-Kate told herself. *No use getting all pushed out of shape over a boy. Or a dance.*

So what if it was the biggest and most fun dance of the whole school year?

She finished eating, then trudged back to her dorm and dragged herself into her room. Ginger was lying on the top bunk, reading. She glanced up as Mary-Kate threw her baseball glove on the floor.

"What's the matter?" Ginger asked.

"Nothing," Mary-Kate lied.

"Hmm." Ginger was silent for a minute. She seemed to be thinking. "Hey, guess what? Our maths test was cancelled. Mr Surinam is sick, so we don't have to go to maths tomorrow. Isn't that great?"

"I guess so," Mary-Kate said with a shrug.

"Well, have you heard the good news?" Ginger asked brightly.

"No. What?"

"Campbell has a date for the dance!" Ginger said. "She just called and told me."

Oh, great, Mary-Kate thought. *Everyone in the whole school has a date! Except Ashley and me.*

But she was happy for Campbell. Sort of.

"That's nice," Mary-Kate said glumly. "Who's she going with?"

"Grant Marino," Ginger said.

"What?" Mary-Kate's mouth fell open. "Are you kidding?" she asked. "I thought *you* liked Grant – not Campbell."

Ginger looked puzzled. "Where did you ever get that idea?"

But Mary-Kate wasn't listening.

I don't believe it! she thought. *How could Campbell do that to me?*

How could she steal the one guy I like?

CHAPTER EIGHT

Mary-Kate ran out of her room. Her heart was pounding and her face was burning hot. She hurried through the lobby of Porter House, zooming for the front door.

"Mary-Kate? Isn't it a bit late to be going out?" Miss Viola called from the door of her room.

Miss Viola was the housemother. Her room was on the first floor of Porter House. She made sure the girls were all inside by 9 p.m., when she locked the front door.

Mary-Kate froze. "I'll be back in time," she answered. Her voice was shaking. "I'm just going next door."

"Well, don't be late," Miss Viola said.

Mary-Kate dashed out of Porter House and along the walkway leading to Phipps.

I don't even know which room Campbell has! she realized as she yanked open the other house's front door.

Inside, just off the lobby, a group of girls were gathered in the lounge. Mary-Kate poked her head in.

"Uh, does anyone know which room Campbell Smith is in?" she asked. "She recently swapped with Ginger Halliday. Jamie Randolph is her roommate."

"Upstairs. First door on the left," someone said.

"Thanks," Mary-Kate said.

Her throat started to tighten as she took the stairs two at a time.

What if she's not there? What if she's out for a walk or something?

Or what if she's on the hall phone right now – talking to Grant?

Mary-Kate got angrier with every step.

By the time she reached Campbell's new room, she felt as if her blood were boiling!

Campbell was sprawled on a rug on the floor, reading her book for English.

"Hello, traitor!" Mary-Kate snapped, standing in

the doorway with her hands on her hips.

Campbell's head shot up with a jerk. "Uh, hi. What's wrong with you?"

"Oh, nothing," Mary-Kate said. "I just can't believe you've stolen the only guy I really liked – that's all!"

"What are you talking about?" Campbell asked.

She dropped her book and sat up, cross-legged. She really did look puzzled.

"Don't play dumb," Mary-Kate cried. "I'm talking about Grant! You're going to the dance with him!"

Then she realized she was almost yelling. She checked over her shoulder to see if anyone had heard her in the hall. The coast was clear. "How could you?" she asked more softly.

"Why shouldn't I go with Grant?" Campbell answered. "You said *you* wouldn't go with him."

I did? When? Mary-Kate thought.

Oh, yeah. In the dining hall.

But that was only because. . . because she didn't think he would ask her!

Mary-Kate felt as if she were going to cry. She didn't want Campbell to see.

"I'm just saying that's not how roommates treat each other," Mary-Kate shot back. Her voice was still shaky. "Not if they're really friends."

Two of a Kind

Then she spun round and stormed out.

Her heart was still pounding as she started down the hall.

The last room on the right, near the stairs, was brightly lit. Mary-Kate could hear voices inside. Even before she got there, she recognized one of the voices. It was Dana Woletsky.

"I just figured, why wait for him to ask me?" Dana was saying. "So I asked him to the dance!"

"And he said yes?" another girl in the room asked.

"Yup. I'm going to the Spring Fling with Ross!" Dana announced.

Ross? Ross Lambert?

Oh, no! Mary-Kate thought. *This is the worst!*

She wanted to crawl under a radiator and hide.

She and Ashley had both been dumped by the guys they liked!

CHAPTER NINE

"Ashley!"

Ashley's head jerked up when she heard her name being hissed. Mary-Kate was standing in her doorway, out of breath. And her face was bright red.

"What's wrong?" Ashley asked.

Mary-Kate leaned into the room and glanced around. "Where's Phoebe?" she asked softly.

"Gone. She's studying with Wendy. Why?" Ashley said.

"Because I don't want to say anything in front of her," Mary-Kate explained. She came in and closed the door behind her. "I have terrible news."

What could be so bad? Ashley wondered. Did it have something to do with the All-Stars baseball team? Ashley knew that Mary-Kate had been practising with the team earlier that day.

"I was just over in Phipps," Mary-Kate began. "And I overheard Dana talking. She and Ross Lambert are going to the dance!"

"Oh, no!" Ashley cried. "She's been trying to get him away from me all week! And it worked. He asked her out."

"No way." Mary-Kate shook her head. "From what I heard, she asked him."

That took a lot of nerve! Ashley thought.

But that was Dana. There was nothing she wouldn't do to get what she wanted.

"I can't believe it," Ashley said. "Dana and Ross are going together – to the biggest dance of the year! I'll be the only person in the whole school going alone!"

"No, you won't," Mary-Kate said. "I don't have a date either." She sat down on Phoebe's bed. "Grant asked Campbell to the Spring Fling. Can you believe that?"

Ashley's mouth fell open. "Campbell? Really?"

Mary-Kate quickly explained what had happened. Ashley saw how miserable she was.

"What are we going to do?" Ashley moaned. "We've been deserted!"

"There's only one thing to do," Mary-Kate replied.

"What?" Ashley held her breath.

"Get revenge!" Mary-Kate joked.

"Good plan!" Ashley agreed. At least it made her feel better to laugh about it. "I have an idea," she said, giggling. "How about if we sneak green food colouring into Dana's shampoo? We could do it next Saturday morning – the day of the dance. Then Dana would be too embarrassed to show up."

"Great idea!" Mary-Kate grinned. "Oh! I've got one! How about this? We make up some excuse to lure Dana and Campbell out of Phipps one night this week. If they don't get back to the house by Lights Out, they'll be grounded. Then they won't be allowed to go to the dance! Or the Lock-In!"

Ashley's eyes twinkled. "That's really too mean!" she said.

Mary-Kate flopped down on Ashley's bed and sighed.

Then Ashley saw Mary-Kate's eyes open wide. Her face was totally serious.

"What?" Ashley asked. "I can tell you've had a brainstorm."

"This is the best plan of all," Mary-Kate said, sitting up and leaning close to her sister, "because it could actually work!"

"What?" Ashley held her breath.

Two of a Kind

"What if we ask Dana to clean up all those weeds that are growing by the back door at the new Student U?" Mary-Kate suggested. "We could tell her the overgrown brush has to be cleared away so the back door can be opened during the dance."

"No way!" Ashley shrieked, laughing. "You know there's poison ivy growing there!"

Mary-Kate jumped up and danced around the room. "I know! Wouldn't that be perfect? Dana would be covered with poison ivy! Then she couldn't come to the dance!"

Ashley laughed and threw a pillow at her sister. "I bet if we asked Campbell to help, she would. Then she'd have to stay home, too."

Mary-Kate laughed and headed towards the door.

"Well, I feel better now," she said. "I think I'll go back to my room" – she lowered her voice – "and face another night with poor, sniffling Ginger."

"Good luck," Ashley whispered sympathetically.

"Anyway, it was a kick to think about revenge," Mary-Kate said. "But we'd never really do anything, right?"

"Right." Ashley nodded.

We'd never actually *get revenge on Dana and Campbell*, Ashley thought.

Would we?

CHAPTER TEN

"Ross, could you help me?" Ashley called across the Student U.

Ross shot her a glare. "What now?" he complained, dragging his feet as he walked towards her.

Gosh, Ashley thought. Why was he in such a grouchy mood?

"All I want to do is move the sofa to the other wall," she said.

"But I just moved it to *that* wall," Ross pointed out.

"Okay, so I've changed my mind a few times," Ashley admitted. "But we have to get the furniture right, so we have room for the dance tomorrow."

Ashley's throat sort of closed up when she said that word. *Dance. I wonder if I'll actually get to do any dancing at the Spring Fling,* she thought.

"Do you need some help?" Mary-Kate asked.

Mary-Kate was working with Samantha and Phoebe on the decorations. They were hanging balloons from the ceiling and stringing small white lights all around the edges of the room.

"I think Ross and I can do it," Ashley answered.

She picked up one end of the sofa – but it was heavy. The legs on her end barely left the ground.

Ross hefted the other end easily. "Talk about not carrying your share of the load!" he teased.

"I'm trying," Ashley said. She almost grunted as she struggled to haul the small leather sofa to the far wall.

But it was too heavy.

She dropped her end with a loud *clunk*. Her side stuck out in the room. Ross's end of the sofa was where it should have been – against the wall.

Ross laughed. "Is that where you want it?" he teased.

Dana laughed. "Very creative, Ashley," she called. "Yeah – I like it. We'll call it the Ashley Burke corner."

Ashley tossed her hair over her shoulder and

tried to ignore the remark. She leant against the sofa and shoved it the rest of the way into place.

"Thanks," she said to Ross.

Ross didn't say anything. He just wandered back to where Dana was standing. Dana muttered something in a low whisper. Ross laughed hard.

Great, Ashley thought. *I bet they're talking about me!*

At least the new Student U looked great. Ashley gazed around with pride. After all their work, it was almost complete. The walls had been freshly painted black and sea-foam green and new lights had been installed – including the mirrored disco ball that Ashley wanted.

One back room held a sofa, VCR, TV, video games, and lots of beanbag chairs. The other back room had the drink and snack machines. A folding rollaway ping-pong table stood against one wall in the big room.

And they had even raised enough money at the car wash to buy the second VCR that Ross wanted. It was in the big room, hooked up to a wide-screen TV.

Best of all, the new furniture had been delivered! Ashley loved it.

The sofas were really cool. There were lots of small love seats covered in salmon-and-white leatherette. They looked like they came right out of a 1950s Chevrolet convertible. And there was a really cool colourful rug in the middle of the room, for sprawling on.

"This place is so amazing!" Mary-Kate said. "I love it!"

"Great balloons," Ashley complimented her sister.

"Grant, can you hand me that masking tape?" Mary-Kate called from a stepladder.

Grant mumbled an answer. He handed her the tape without even looking her in the eye.

Wow, Ashley thought. Grant was being so cold to Mary-Kate! Ashley couldn't figure out why. Mary-Kate had always been nice to Grant!

And Ross acted totally icy toward Ashley. She could tell he thought she was bossy. But that was no reason to be so rude!

Going to the dance was going to be torture.

"We've got to roll up the rug," Ashley announced. She tried not to look in Ross's direction.

He looked annoyed anyhow. "I've just unrolled it – right before you got here," Ross complained.

"Well, we have to roll it up again for the dance," Ashley explained patiently. She glanced round, looking for a place to put it. Mary-Kate was still on the ladder, so they couldn't move the rug yet.

Likes Me, Likes Me Not

"Over there in that corner," she said, pointing. "But wait till Mary-Kate's finished decorating."

"Whatever." Ross turned away.

Ashley swallowed hard. She hated how Ross was talking to her. But she didn't want it to show. And most of all, she didn't want Dana to know she was jealous. She had better behave as if everything was okay.

Ashley stood and stared at the black wall. "You know, that was a great idea," she said to Ross. "One black wall. I'm really glad we did it."

"You mean I did do something right?" he said in a sarcastic voice.

Gosh! Ashley thought. Her face fell. *I'm trying to be nice, and he's yelling at me!*

Her eyes met Mary-Kate's.

Uh-oh, Ashley thought. *Mary-Kate looks furious!*

"Ross?" Mary-Kate called from the ladder. "There's still one thing you guys need to do. Why don't you and Grant go outside – and pull all those weeds that are growing by the back door!"

Oh, no! Ashley thought. *The poison ivy!*

"No!" she blurted out. "Don't do it!"

"Why not?" Ross snapped. "What's wrong – are you afraid we won't do it right?"

Everyone in the room stared at Ashley. She gulped and said, "No that's not it. Mary-Kate doesn't know it but there's poison ivy out there and—"

"Come on, I'll help you, Ross," Grant interrupted her. He sounded grumpy. "Let's just do it and get it over with."

"No!" Ashley called again. "Let it go. We don't need to open that door."

But it was too late. The guys had already marched out of the front door and round the building. They were pulling the weeds – with their bare hands and arms!

Yikes! Ashley thought. *They're going to be covered with poison ivy. And it will be all our fault!*

CHAPTER ELEVEN

"Where are they?" Ashley whispered to Mary-Kate.

Ashley glanced at her watch. It was 4.30 p.m. the next afternoon. Both sisters stood in the new Student U, setting up the table for refreshments. "Ross and Grant were supposed to be here an hour ago."

Mary-Kate gulped. "Poison ivy?" she guessed.

"That's what I'm afraid of," Ashley said nervously. "You never should have sent them out to pull those weeds."

"I know!" Mary-Kate buried her face in her hands. "But I couldn't help it. I just snapped when I heard Ross talking to you that way. He was being so. . . so mean!"

"Well, Grant was pretty cold to you, too," Ashley said. "Maybe that's why you snapped."

"Maybe," Mary-Kate admitted. She spread a paper tablecloth out on the table. Then she started lining up paper cups for the drinks. "But I'll still feel guilty if they actually get poison ivy."

"Well, maybe they're just sick of doing all the grunt work," Ashley said. She glanced at her watch again. "Do you think Ross and Grant would really just not show? I mean, if they were healthy, they'd be here – wouldn't they?"

Ashley bit her fingernail and glanced around. There wasn't much left to do. All the decorations were in place. The crisps and snacks were lined up on the counter in the small back room. Everything was ready.

She looked at her watch again.

"That's the fourth time you've checked your watch," Mary-Kate said. "Give up. They're not coming."

"I know," Ashley said. "But how can we find out if it's because they're slackers – or because they're itching like crazy?"

Mary-Kate thought for a minute. Her eyes lit up. "Brainstorm," she said. "We'll call Jeremy. He can find out what's going on!"

Likes Me, Likes Me Not

Good idea, Ashley thought. Jeremy was their cousin and a student at Harrington. He could definitely find out if Ross and Grant had poison ivy.

The twins hurried back to Porter House. But there was only one phone in the dorm – in the hall. And seven girls were already waiting to use it!

"We made a sign-up sheet," Elise Van Hook explained.

"How come?" Ashley asked. "I thought we weren't allowed to do that."

"Miss Viola said it was okay, just for tonight—because so many girls want to call guys at Harrington. Everyone's trying to get a last-minute date for the dance tomorrow. Put your name here, and you don't have to queue for the phone." She handed Ashley a clipboard.

"Okay," Ashley said, signing her name. "Thanks. We'll wait anyhow."

Both girls sat down on the stairs. Forty minutes passed. Finally Elise called Ashley's name.

"Coming!" Ashley said, jumping up.

Mary-Kate followed her.

Ashley dialled the dorm at Harrington. She asked for Jeremy.

"Hi," Jeremy said. "What's up? You guys need dates for the dance or something?"

"No," Ashley said, talking softly so the other girls in the hall wouldn't hear. "Listen, we need a favour."

Quickly Ashley explained to Jeremy that she wanted him to go spy on Grant and Ross to find out if they were ill... or had any "rashes".

And she made him promise not to tell anyone why he was doing it!

"I'll hold," Ashley said. "Hurry."

Ashley tapped her fingers nervously while she waited.

"Are you talking or not?" a girl asked. "Because I'm next for the phone."

"I'm talking," Ashley said.

"Doesn't sound like it," the girl said.

"Okay, I'm waiting to finish talking," Ashley explained. *Hurry up, Jeremy!* she thought.

"Hi," he finally said, back on the line. "Good news. Ross and Grant are fine."

"They are? I mean, no signs of... anything?" she asked.

"Like what?" Jeremy said. "I mean, they're both playing video games in the common room. They don't look ill at all."

"They're not itching or anything?" Ashley whispered into the phone. "No signs of poison ivy?"

"Nope," Jeremy said. "Not that I could see. Why? What's going on?"

"Never mind," Ashley said. "See you later, okay?"

"Wait!" Jeremy yelled. "Don't hang up!"

"What?" Ashley asked.

"I heard that you don't have a date for the Spring Fling," he said. "So I was wondering, do you want me to fix you up with Brian Maloney?"

Brian Maloney? Was he kidding? Brian was the creepiest kid at Harrington!

"No thanks." Ashley said. "Goodbye!" She hung the phone up and pulled Mary-Kate aside. "He tried to fix me up with Brian Maloney!"

"Ew," Mary-Kate said. "He must think you're desperate!" She leant close to Ashley. "What did he say about you-know-who?" she whispered.

"Oh – they're fine," Ashley answered. "Nothing wrong."

"That's good," Mary-Kate said. "I suppose."

The twins were quiet as they wandered back to Ashley's room.

"So why didn't they come to the Student U today?" Mary-Kate wondered.

"Because they didn't want to be with us?" Ashley guessed out loud.

Two of a Kind

Mary-Kate shrugged. "I suppose so," she said softly.

"It's going to be no fun at the dance tomorrow night," Ashley said. "We'll have to watch them spend the whole night dancing with Dana and Campbell."

"No kidding," Mary-Kate said. "And then we'll probably have to spend the rest of the night at the Lock-In – listening to Dana talk about what a fabulous guy Ross is."

Yikes, Ashley thought. *That would be torture!*

In fact, it was more than Ashley could take.

"No, we don't," Ashley declared firmly.

"Huh? Why not?" Mary-Kate said. "What are you going to do – wear blinders and earplugs?"

"No," Ashley announced. "I'm not going to go. I'm going to skip the dance and the Lock-In altogether!"

CHAPTER TWELVE

"You guys are nuts," Phoebe said to Mary-Kate and Ashley the next night. "You're missing out on the biggest dance of the year! Are you really going to stay here? Alone? All night?"

"We're not alone," Mary-Kate joked. "We have Ginger."

She nodded towards her own room, down the hall.

"Oh, right," Phoebe said, rolling her eyes. "She's allergic to dancing or something?"

"Something," Mary-Kate answered glumly. "Anyway, she's staying in her room tonight. Our room, I should say. So we won't be alone."

"Whatever," Phoebe said. "But I still say you're nuts."

"We'll have more fun staying in," Ashley insisted. "We're going to make popcorn and watch films all night."

"That's what we're doing at the Lock-In!" Phoebe reminded her. "At least you could come to that – when the dance is over."

"No thanks," Mary-Kate said.

She tried to sound okay about it, but it was a struggle. Missing out on a big dance was not Mary-Kate's idea of a great time. But she had decided to go along with Ashley. Neither girl thought it would be fun to go to the dance.

"Well, if you're not going, can I borrow your shawl?" Phoebe asked Ashley.

Ashley nodded and reached into her cupboard. Her black silk shawl with embroidery and fringe was hanging there.

"Yeah – this will look great with your black dress," Ashley said. "Here. Have fun."

"Yeah. You, too." Phoebe walked out of the door.

Mary-Kate listened to Phoebe's footsteps on the stairs. They echoed because the house was so empty.

"This is the pits," she said when they were finally alone.

"I know," Ashley said. "It's so quiet in here! But I'm still glad we're doing it. I just couldn't stand to watch Ross dance with Dana all night."

"Ditto for Grant," Mary-Kate said.

"What? You think Grant will dance all night with Dana, too?" Ashley was trying to make a joke. But Mary-Kate could tell her heart wasn't in it.

Mary-Kate sighed. "Come on. We need a movie. Let's hit the common room." Mary-Kate jumped off Ashley's bed and headed for the door.

But Ashley didn't budge. "I've seen all the ones in the common room," she mumbled glumly.

"Me, too," Mary-Kate admitted. She stood in the doorway, thinking. "I know! Ginger's got a copy of *Jaws*. We could watch that again."

"Okay," Ashley said with a nod. "It's better than nothing."

"I'll go and get it," Mary-Kate said.

She slipped her feet into her slippers and padded down the hall. Ginger was sitting at her desk, writing a letter.

"Hi," Mary-Kate said. "Can we borrow *Jaws*?"

Ginger glanced up, as if she had been startled. "Uh, sure," she said. She stared at Mary-Kate's clothes. "But aren't you going to the dance?"

"Nope," Mary-Kate answered. "Ashley and I are boycotting it."

"How come?" Ginger asked. She swivelled in her

chair to face Mary-Kate, and gave her a worried glance.

Wow, Mary-Kate thought. *She looks like she really cares!* For the first time, Mary-Kate felt like opening up to Ginger. Maybe because the house seemed so lonely.

Or maybe it's because I miss Campbell, Mary-Kate thought.

Anyway, Mary-Kate decided to tell Ginger the truth.

"I just couldn't face it," she admitted.

"Face what?" Ginger asked.

"Grant," Mary-Kate answered. "You know how you kept asking me if I liked him? Well, I do. But he's taking Campbell to the dance instead."

"You're kidding!" Ginger's eyes opened wide. "Why didn't you tell me before?"

"Because I didn't want it getting all over school," Mary-Kate said.

"But he likes *you!*" Ginger almost squealed.

"He does? No way!" Mary-Kate said.

"Yes, he does," Ginger insisted. "He told Campbell that he liked you – and asked her to find out if you liked him. That was the day she moved into my old room."

"No way," Mary-Kate said again. But her heart

was beating fast. Could it possibly be true?

"Definitely," Ginger said. "But since Campbell wasn't going to be here to pick your brains, she asked me to find out if you liked him. That's why I kept asking you."

"Ohmigosh!" Mary-Kate blurted out. "I thought you were just being nosy!"

Or that maybe you liked Grant yourself, Mary-Kate thought.

Ginger flinched, but Mary-Kate ran over and gave her a hug.

"I'm sorry," she said. "I didn't mean it that way."

"That's okay," Ginger said. "I suppose it did seem a little bit like I was just fishing for gossip. But I wasn't."

"Oh, no." Mary-Kate's eyes opened wide. She remembered what happened in the dining hall. "Campbell asked me about him, too."

"I know," Ginger said. "I heard all about it from Jamie. Anyway, Campbell told Grant what you said – that you wouldn't go to the dance with him if he asked you. That's why he finally gave up on you and decided to ask Campbell to the dance instead."

Mary-Kate's head was swimming. She didn't know what to say. So that's why Grant was acting so cold to her! He thought she didn't like him!

Two of a Kind

I've been such a jerk! Mary-Kate thought. *Especially for being mad at Campbell, who didn't steal Grant after all!*

"So anyway, you wanted to borrow *Jaws*?" Ginger asked, getting it from her bookshelf.

"No thanks," Mary-Kate said, snapping out of it. "But I wouldn't mind borrowing your earrings. I think I'm going to the dance!"

CHAPTER THIRTEEN

"Okay, I'll go to the dance, too," Ashley said when she heard the whole story from Mary-Kate. "But we're not staying for the Lock-In. Right?"

"Why not?" Mary-Kate asked.

"Because I still don't want to spend the whole night listening to Dana tell me how cool Ross is!" Ashley explained.

"Fine. Just hurry up and get dressed," Mary-Kate begged. "I'll meet you downstairs in ten minutes!"

Ashley glanced in her cupboard. The dress she had been planning to wear to the dance was hanging right at the front.

Quickly she slipped out of her black capri pants and into the little blue chiffon dress.

In two secs, she brushed her hair and tied it into a twisty knot on top of her head. She swiped some lip gloss onto her lips and added a small silver chain necklace.

Perfect! And in only 9.5 minutes – record time!

She met Mary-Kate at the bottom of the stairs. The girls knocked on Miss Viola's door to sign out.

"All right," Miss Viola said. "But if you're not staying for the Lock-In, I'll expect you back here by midnight."

"We'll be back," Ashley promised as they headed out of the door.

The night was chilly, but the stars overhead twinkled brightly. Both girls walked quickly to get out of the cold. It wasn't far to the new Student U. Ashley could see the mirrored disco ball inside, twirling and sparkling with the music.

"I'm glad we're going," Mary-Kate said. "Listen to that! It sounds like everyone's having so much fun!"

"Easy for you to say," Ashley moaned. "Now that you know Grant likes you – you'll have a great time. Ross isn't talking to me."

Mary-Kate gave Ashley a little squeeze on the arm. "Come on," she said. "It'll be okay. I've got to find Campbell and apologise to her."

Likes Me, Likes Me Not

The girls stepped into the new Student U and gazed round. The dance was in full swing. But Ashley didn't see anyone she knew at first.

Then she made out a familiar face on the other side of the room. "There she is!" Ashley called out.

"What?" Mary-Kate asked, yelling to be heard above the loud music.

"There's Campbell," Ashley yelled back.

Ashley watched as Mary-Kate threaded her way through the crowd. Campbell and Grant were standing together on the far side of the room. Ashley couldn't hear, but she saw Mary-Kate take Campbell aside. The two girls talked for a minute, then hugged.

Good, Ashley thought. *They've patched it up.*

Just then Ashley felt someone tap her on the shoulder.

"Want to dance?" Brian Maloney asked her.

Ashley checked him out quickly. Brian looked a lot better than she remembered him. But she wasn't in the mood.

"Uh, I can't right now. I've got to talk to my sister," she told him.

Ashley slipped away and made her way round the edge of the room towards Mary-Kate and Campbell. But just as she got there, Mary-Kate and

Two of a Kind

Grant walked out onto the dance floor together.

That's great, Ashley thought. A slow dance was playing. She watched her sister dancing cheek to cheek with Grant. Mary-Kate wrapped her arms round his neck.

"Hi," Campbell said, smiling. "What's up?"

"You tell me," Ashley said. "It looks like you handed Grant over to my sister."

"I did. I didn't really want to be with him, anyway," Campbell said. "He's been talking about Mary-Kate the whole night."

"Really?" Ashley felt a little bit jealous.

"Yeah," Campbell said. "He really likes her. So I told them to go ahead and dance."

"That's so nice," Ashley said. But her face was sort of sad.

"What's wrong with you?" Campbell asked.

Ashley sighed. "Umm, I don't know. I just sort of wish I was here with someone," Ashley admitted.

"Who?" Campbell asked. "Anyone in particular?"

Should I tell her? Ashley wondered. *Oh, why not!*

"Ross," Ashley said, speaking into Campbell's ear. "But don't tell anyone. He doesn't like me. He likes Dana."

"Whoa!" Campbell said. She looked totally shocked. "You mean you don't hate him?"

Ashley shook her head. "Why would I hate him?"

"Well, it's just that I've heard Dana talking to him on the phone," Campbell said. "You know – she lives right down the hall from me in Phipps. She's been telling him stuff about you for the past two weeks."

"What? What kind of stuff?" Ashley demanded, grabbing Campbell's arm.

"Okay, I'll tell you," Campbell said. "But let's go outside. It's too loud in here!"

The girls slipped out of the back door, and stood shivering in the cold. Quickly Campbell explained what she had heard Dana say to Ross.

"Dana kept telling him that you thought he was lazy," Campbell said. "And that you complained about his ideas for the Student U all the time, behind his back."

"I don't believe it!" Ashley cried. "She's such a liar! None of that is true!"

"Believe it," Campbell said. "I mean, two nights ago I heard her tell him that you spent the whole lunch break knocking his taste in music."

"No wonder he's been so mean to me!" Ashley said, heading back inside.

"What do you think you're going to do?"

Two of a Kind

Campbell called, following her into the Student U.

"What can I do?" Ashley asked. "I can't tell him the truth. He'd never believe me. But at least I can get the disc jockey to stop playing that slow dance – so I don't have to watch Dana and Ross dance so close together!"

Ashley stomped through the crowd to where the DJ was sitting. She leant over and shouted to be heard.

"Could you play something by 4 You next?" she asked.

"Sure," the DJ said. "What's your name?"

Why would he want to know my name? she wondered. But she told him anyhow.

"Okay," he said. "You got it, Ashley Burke."

A minute later, the slow song stopped. Ross and Dana were only a few feet away. Then a new song by 4 You started blaring out of the speaker system.

"This one is by request – for Ashley Burke," the DJ said.

Ashley blushed as a crowd of people turned to stare at her. *I'm not even dancing!* she thought. She felt completely stupid.

Then Ross caught her eye. He walked towards her. "You asked for 4 You?" he said. "I thought you hated them."

"No," she said, gazing into his eyes. "I love them. There are a lot of things I like that you don't know about."

Ross looked confused. "Really?" he asked.

Ashley nodded. "Dana has been telling you things about me that aren't true," she added. "In fact, I'll bet nothing she said about me is true."

Ross stared at her hard. Then he glanced at Dana. Then back at Ashley.

"Can we talk about this while we dance?" he asked.

"Definitely!" Ashley said, smiling so hard it almost hurt.

They stepped on to the dance floor and started moving to the music. But they couldn't really talk. The music was too loud. When the song ended, Ross reached out and grabbed Ashley's hand.

"Wait," he said. "Stay until there's a slow dance."

Ashley's heart flipped over. "What about Dana?" she asked.

"Forget Dana," Ross said.

Ashley saw Dana glaring at her and Ross. Then she whirled around and stomped away. She tossed her hair over her shoulders as she marched to the small room with the drink machines.

Then Ross took Ashley's hand and started dancing.

Two of a Kind

A slow song was playing. Ashley stood close to him and put her arms round his neck.

This is so cool! she thought. Ashley looked around the room. She saw Mary-Kate and Grant. They were slow-dancing, too.

"So you didn't tell Dana you thought I was lazy?" Ross asked. He reached up and scratched his neck.

"No way!" Ashley said. "You worked harder on this place than anyone."

"Not harder than you," he said. "I thought we made a great team."

He pulled her close to him.

Ashley beamed. This was a fantastic night!

When the song was over, they went to get something to drink. Then they played a few video games in the back room. And then they danced five more dances together.

Ashley couldn't believe it. And she couldn't wait to tell Phoebe and Mary-Kate all about it!

"Are you going to keep the disco ball going during the Lock-In?" Ross asked.

"The Lock-In?" Ashley's eyes popped. "I forgot about the Lock-In!"

"Huh? How could you forget about it?" Ross asked.

Likes Me, Likes Me Not

"Oh, Mary-Kate and I weren't going to stay for it," Ashley explained quickly. "We didn't bring our sleeping bags. What time is it – do you know?"

Ross glanced at his watch. "Eleven forty-five," he said. "The dance is almost over."

"Oh, no! Could you excuse me?" Ashley cried.

Ross nodded, and Ashley dashed across the room to find her sister.

"The Lock-In!" she said, grabbing Mary-Kate's arm. "We've got to stay for it!"

"But we don't have time to get our stuff!" Mary-Kate said. "They'll lock the doors of the Student U at midnight!"

"I don't care. We've got to try!" Ashley cried. "Come on – let's run!"

CHAPTER FOURTEEN

Mary-Kate said a quick goodnight to Grant. Ashley hurried to do the same with Ross. Then the girls raced out of the front door of the Student U and ran across the dark school yard.

"We'll never get back in time!" Mary-Kate called to Ashley, who was in the lead.

"We have to!" Ashley said. "I don't want to miss it. This is going to be the best night of the year!"

A few minutes later, the twins reached the front door of Porter House. They were both panting and out of breath.

"The door's locked!" Mary-Kate cried, pulling on the handle.

"Ring the bell!" Ashley said.

Likes Me, Likes Me Not

Mary-Kate pushed on the buzzer. Twice.

"Hurry up, Miss Viola," Ashley muttered.

Finally the front door opened. Mary-Kate ran in and took the steps two at a time.

"Ah. You just made it," Miss Viola said, glancing at the big grandfather clock in the lobby.

"We're going to go back to the Lock-In," Ashley said, talking fast and trying to get past the housemother. "We've got to get our sleeping bags and pyjamas. Excuse me, Miss Viola."

"Oh, no you're not!" Miss Viola said. "It's too late. You'll never get back there before they lock the doors."

Ashley glanced at the clock. It was five minutes to midnight.

"Oh, please, Miss Viola! Please! We'll run!" Ashley said.

"No, I'm afraid not," the housemother said. "How will I know if you made it? I don't want you out there alone, especially if you're locked out."

But then Miss Viola glanced out of the window. Her face changed. "Well," she said, "I see Fred, the night guard out there. Maybe he could escort you. And if the doors are locked—"

"Great!" Ashley said, dashing up the stairs before Miss Viola finished her sentence.

Two of a Kind

Ashley raced into her room, grabbed her pyjamas and sleeping bag, and ran out. She didn't even bother to put her pyjamas in a bag. There was no time!

"Come on!" Ashley called to Mary-Kate down the hall.

"I'm already downstairs!" Mary-Kate yelled up from the bottom. "And look who's coming with us!"

Ashley almost slipped, she was running so fast to get down the stairs.

"Who?" she asked.

"Ginger!" Mary-Kate said. "Isn't that great?"

"Definitely!" Ashley said, giving Ginger a big smile.

"I'm fed up with being ill," Ginger announced. "Who cares if I sneeze all night? I've got tissues."

"Way to go!" Mary-Kate said.

Ashley glanced at the grandfather clock. It said one minute to midnight.

Fred was standing in the lobby.

"Thank you, Miss Viola!" Ashley called as she raced past Fred, out of the front door. "Come on, Fred!"

Fred laughed as he slowly followed the three girls into the night. "You go on ahead," he called. "I can see you okay."

Likes Me, Likes Me Not

That's what we were planning to do! Ashley thought as she started to run.

Both twins were dragging their sleeping bags and pyjamas on the ground. But Ashley didn't care. She just didn't want to be left out of all the fun!

When they were only halfway there, Ashley heard the clock tower chiming.

Midnight.

No! she thought. *Don't lock the doors yet! Please!*

A minute and a half later, they reached the front door of the Student U. The building was still all lit up inside.

And the front door was wide open!

Mrs Pritchard stood near it, trying to get the last of the boys to leave.

"Come on, boys!" she called. "The shuttle bus for Harrington is ready to pull away! Let's go!"

Ashley and Mary-Kate exchanged high fives.

"We made it!" Mary-Kate cheered.

"Yes!" Ginger cheered, running to catch up.

Ashley turned to wave at Fred. Then all three girls slipped inside.

"Well, hello!" Mrs Pritchard said to them. "I'm glad to see you've decided to join us! You, too, Ginger. And congratulations, Ashley. Your committee did a good job with this building. You should be proud."

"Thank you. I am," Ashley said. When Mrs Pritchard turned away, Ashley leant to whisper in her sister's ear. "Isn't this an awesome night?"

"Completely!" Mary-Kate said. "And it's just getting started!"

Ashley found a good spot for her sleeping bag near Phoebe's and spread it out on the floor. Mary-Kate put hers next to Campbell's.

Ginger hurried to find her old roommate, Jamie.

For the next few hours, the girls did nothing but talk about the dance. And eat! Ashley was starving. She gobbled down two pieces of pizza and drank two cokes. Then she started on the crisps.

"Look at Dana," Phoebe whispered. "She's over there pouting – even though she's surrounded by all her friends."

"I don't even care about Dana any more!" Ashley declared. "This was one of the best nights of my life."

When Ashley and her friends had all finished talking about the dance, they moved into the back room to watch a movie. Then they played a game of Truth or Dare. Then they started on the snacks again.

By five in the morning, Ashley was pretty tired. But she wasn't going to sleep. Not until the Lock-In was over!

Likes Me, Likes Me Not

She glanced at Mary-Kate, who was snoozing on her sleeping bag.

What a great night, Ashley thought.

Some of the other girls were sleeping, too. Ashley took out her diary and wrote in it. All about Ross, and the dance, and the Lock-In.

Then she lay on her stomach and watched the sun starting to come up.

This is the best, she thought. The only thing she could possibly complain about was her pyjamas. They were itchy. She reached down and scratched both arms.

But the more she scratched, the more she itched.

Maybe I'm allergic to my roommate, too! she thought. *Just like Ginger!*

Then she noticed Mary-Kate scratching in her sleep.

She was rubbing her arms, too. Ashley got up and crept over to Mary-Kate's sleeping bag. She stared at her sister's arms.

Oh, no! Ashley thought.

"Mary-Kate, wake up!" Ashley said, shaking her sister.

Mary-Kate slowly opened her eyes. "What?" she mumbled groggily.

"Bad news!" Ashley said. "I think we have poison ivy! Look at your arms. We probably got it from dancing with the guys!"

Mary-Kate sat bolt upright.

"You're kidding!" she said. She stared at her arms. They were both bumpy and red. Her eyes opened wide. "Oh, man. The guys probably have it on their necks. They're probably scratching right now, too!"

"Shhh!" someone scolded them from a sleeping bag nearby. "I'm trying to sleep!"

Ashley tried not to scratch. But her arms were driving her crazy.

"Oh, well," Ashley said. "Perhaps we deserve it."

"Yeah? Well, at least we aren't the only ones. Guess who else deserves it?" Mary-Kate said with a smile.

Ashley followed her sister's stare.

There, on the other side of the room, was Dana.

Lying in her sleeping bag.

Scratching!

 # ACORN

The Voice of White Oak Academy Since 1905

SQUEAKY CLEAN!
by Elise Van Hook

Watch out, Porter House! You have a new resident – and it's got a long tail and little grey whiskers!!

The new tenant – a mouse! – moved in a few days ago. She was first seen in the old warehouse at the north end of the school yard. Mary-Kate Burke spotted the little squeaker during the clean-up session last week. Dana Woletsky immediately voted to set a mousetrap. But Phoebe Cahill, a long-time animal-lover, decided to catch the mouse instead. She set a "kind animal" trap – and brought the mouse to Porter House the next day.

Here's the problem. The door to the trap was loose – and the mouse escaped.

Now there's a mouse in Porter House!

Miss Viola was heard saying, "It isn't the first mouse and it won't be the last." Other Porter House residents were heard to reply, "Eek!"

GLAM GAB
by Ashley Burke and Phoebe Cahill

Fashion expert Ashley Burke

What's the latest fashion trend? Beads, beads, beads! If your clothes aren't already bead-decked, don't worry. It's easy to add some beaded beauty to an old pair

of jeans, a skirt, or even a scrunchie. Here's how:

You will need: 1) a piece of clothing; 2) a needle and thread to match the colour of the garment; 3) beaded trim by the metre from a fabric shop OR tiny beads and clear nylon thread from a craft shop.

If you are using beaded trim by the metre: Buy enough trim by the metre to go all the way around your skirt or trouser legs, with a one inch overlap.

Sew the trim to the hem of the garment, using matching thread. Begin and end near a seam. Overlap the trim and fold the top end under itself.

If you are using beads and clear nylon thread:
Make a knot in the nylon thread and pull the thread through from the wrong side of the garment. Add a few beads and take another small stitch. Add a few more beads and take more stitches until you have sewn all the way around.

To add dangling beads:
Sew a few beads on to the hem of the garment, as above. Then string one inch of beads on to the nylon thread without taking a stitch into the

material. Loop the thread around the outside of the last bead to make a knot. Push the thread back up through the remaining inch-long section of beads. Now you have a beaded dangle. Continue sewing beads across the hem, adding one-inch dangles every half inch as you go.

Wear your beaded beauty to the Spring Fling and show everyone how cool beads are!

THE GET-REAL GIRL

Dear Get-Real Girl,
The girls who live in the room next door are driving me nuts. Every Friday night they order pizzas for about ten girls. They crank the stereo so loud, I can't get any homework done! How can I make them shut up?
Signed,
Cranky Neighbour

Dear Cranky,
Puh-lease! You're trying to do homework on a Friday

night? Get real! You aren't mad at your next-door-dormies for playing the

stereo too loud. You're jealous that they're having such a blast and you're not invited!

Instead of being a party pooper, why not offer to host the bash in your

room. That way you can clean up the pizza crumbs for a change. And don't forget to invite the girls who live on the other side of you, too – or you'll be reading another letter just like this in my column next month!

                Signed,
                Get-Real Girl

Dear Get-Real Girl,
A few weeks ago this guy from Harrington asked me to the Spring Fling. I said yes because I figured no one else would ask me. Now a different guy wants to ask me to the dance. Guy No. 2 is sooo cute! How can I get out of the first date?
                Signed,
                Desperate

Dear Desperate,
There's a really easy way to get out of the first date. Just tell everyone that you were willing to dump one guy for another – and no one will want to go out with you!

Seriously, it's not worth treating guys like dirt

unless you're willing to be treated the same way in

return. So keep your promises and go with Guy No. 1. But that doesn't mean you can't dance a few times with Cutie No.2. Just remember: Hands off Cutie No.47. He belongs to me!
Signed,
Get-Real Girl

THE FIRST FORM BUZZ
by Dana Woletsky

Well, you know spring has arrived when the gossip is flying as fast as the pollen here at White Oak!

For starters, has anyone noticed that all the daisies here have been picked? Someone whose initials

are AB is playing the "He likes me, likes me not," game. Or did her twin sister pick all the daisies? Hard to tell them apart – since they're both losing in the dating game these days!

We have one big winner at White Oak, though. A certain girl from Porter House recently moved into Phipps – and she wins my award for the Most Boring Wardrobe! Seriously, CS, how can you tell your pyjamas from

your day clothes? Try wearing something other than a baseball jersey for a change!

The hottest rumour of the week is about SS, who claims she can't sit down

in class this week because she hurt her back in a soccer game. But the real scoop is that she stayed under her tanning lamp so long, she burned the backs of her legs to a crisp! I told you it was a hot rumour!

That's it for the buzz. Remember my motto: if you want the scoop, you just gotta snoop!

ALL-STARS SHINE IN STELLAR BALL GAME
by Mary-Kate Burke

Sports pro Mary-Kate Burke

Let's hear a cheer for the White Oak/Harrington All-Stars baseball team! We beat the Danville Day School 3-2 in extra innings last Saturday – a game that is sure to become a White Oak legend.

Both teams came out swinging in the first innings. Danville was up by one when yours truly stepped up to the plate – and slammed a homer!

The score was 2-2 for the next nine innings! The crowd was tense until

Grant Marino stepped up to bat at the top of the tenth. We held our breath. And he slammed another home run straight over the fence to win the game!

Coach Fisher gave Grant the MVP award. And one of his teammates (I'm not saying who) was heard to say, "Hey – he'll always be the Most Valuable Person as far as I'm concerned!"

UPCOMING CALENDAR
Spring/Summer

Take the plunge and come out to cheer for all those cute Harrington guys at

their final platform diving meet on 5 May. It's a totally wet and wild event! (Can anyone say Speedos?)

Don't tell the ants. . . but everyone else is invited to the end-of-school picnic

on 29 May! There will be a prize for the winner of the pie-eating contest. Dress for a mess!

Time to pack it in! Remember: you must have your clothes packed to ship home by

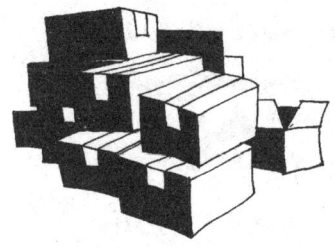

Friday, 25 May. Need extra boxes? Don't go postal! Just ask Mr Frangianella for help.

Something's fishy in the Florida Keys! Find out about a cool summer programme, swimming and snorkelling

till your skin turns wrinkly! Info meeting on Satur-day, 5 May , in the new Student U. Be there – and you'll get hooked for sure!

It's All in the Stars
Spring Horoscopes

Taurus
(20 April–20 May)

Look out, world – here comes the sign of the bull! You're a powerhouse of strength, Taurus. That means you can master anything you decide to tackle this month. Just remember that you can be a little bit stubborn and bull-headed at times – even with your closest friends. Make sure you leave room for someone else's opinion once in a while.

Gemini
(21 May–20 June)

As the school year ends, it's time for a change. How about taking up a new hobby, getting a different haircut, or trying a new food? Take a risk this summer: learn how to juggle, do a back dive, or stand on your head. You'll be surprised how great it feels to look at the world from a different angle!

Cancer
(21 June–22 July)

Your sun sign says you're ready to kick back, relax, and have a rock 'n' roll summer! And hey – that's totally you. You're solid as a rock and always ready to roll with the punches. No wonder your friends like to lean on you. But remember you don't always have to be the strong one. It's okay to depend on somebody else from time to time.

Shore Thing

by Judy Katschke

HarperCollins*Entertainment*
An Imprint of HarperCollins*Publishers*
A PARACHUTE PRESS BOOK

Chapter 1

Saturday

Dear Diary,

Sorry if my handwriting is a little jerky, but I'm sitting on this bus rolling down something called the 100-Mile Highway in Florida. And the last time I checked we still had about fifty-five miles to go.

See, my twin sister Ashley and I are on this really cool school trip. I know, I know – it's the first week of summer vacation. But when I tell you all about this trip you'll see why Ashley and I decided to stick around. Oh, and since you're a brand-new diary (my old one filled up pretty fast), I'll clue you in on all the details.

Ashley and I are First Formers at a boarding school called The White Oak Academy for Girls in New Hampshire. First Form is the school's way of saying seventh grade. That took some getting used to. So did eating oatmeal every morning for breakfast, another White Oak tradition. Just like these summer vacation school trips.

There's a camping trip to Maine, a sightseeing trip to New York City, and a trip to a tiny island off the coast of Florida in an area called the Keys.

Ashley and I chose to spend two weeks on the island at Camp Coral Reef. Then we'll be going to Miami for a week on the beach.

I know what you're thinking, Diary. That Ashley and I are off to roast hot dogs and paint ceramic frogs in arts and crafts. NOT! In this camp we'll learn all about marine biology – fancy words for fish and underwater plants. We're also going to try our hands at wildlife photography, deep sea fishing, and scuba diving.

Diary, when I heard about the scuba diving I was so there. But Ashley needed a little convincing. . .

"You mean I'll have to wear a mask and flippers, and an oxygen tank?" Ashley asked me when I read the brochure out loud.

"Sure!" I said. "How else are you going to get up-close and personal with a barracuda?"

"I'm not sure I want to," Ashley said.

No kidding! Ashley and I may be twins but we're as different as two snowflakes. I dig sports,  drama, and watching the Cubs game in my track-suit. Ashley likes ballet, boys, and clothes, clothes, clothes! Get the picture?

Shore Thing

I can't wait to scuba dive! Of course, we have to get our scuba certificates first, but no problem! I beat Ashley at holding our breaths in the bathtub when we were little.

Now here's the neatest part: some of our best buds from school are going to Camp Coral Reef, too.

"What made you sign up, Cheryl?" I asked during breakfast on our last day of school.

"Are you kidding?" Cheryl Miller said. "After being in New England all winter, I want as much sun as I can get!"

"So do I!" Summer Sorenson said. "I want to kick up my tan before I go home to Malibu. It's definitely fading."

Everyone looked at Summer as if she were from outer space. Her tan will never fade. It's for life!

As for Elise Van Hook, she wants to study marine animals before visiting her Peace Corps volunteer parents in Fiji.

"So you can learn to recognise the natural wildlife?" Ashley asked Elise.

Elise nodded. "I definitely need to know what's poisonous and what's not!" she said.

Two of a Kind Diaries

And then there's Phoebe Cahill. Phoebe is Ashley's roommate and the editor of the First Form newspaper, the *White Oak Acorn*. She loves poetry, classic movies, and vintage clothes. But *not* sports. In fact, Phoebe's idea of the great outdoors is an open-air flea market.

"If you're not a sports nut, why are you going to Florida?" I asked Phoebe. "It's all about water sports!"

"I'm going to write about the trip for the fall issue of the *Acorn*," Phoebe said. "I don't intend to get anywhere near a scuba tank."

"Lucky you," I heard Ashley mutter.

And if you're wondering about boys – some First Formers from the Harrington School for Boys are going, too. Like our cousin Jeremy Burke, who's dying to learn scuba diving. I'm not surprised. He's been blowing bubbles in his milk since he was in kindergarten.

Other Harrington guys are Seth Samuels, Justin Martinez, and Ross Lambert. Ashley has had a crush on Ross since we started White Oak. And after kissing him in the school play, that crush became more of a – CRUNCH! Ashley and Ross had sort of a misunderstanding this spring. But now they're a couple again.

Shore Thing

Ashley is sitting next to me writing in her diary and eating the honey roasted nuts we got on the plane to Miami. She has this serious look on her face as if she's writing a term paper. What's her problem?

Anyway, Diary, gotta go. Jeremy just tossed a rubber cockroach on my lap. And it's time to get even!

Dear Diary,

What was I thinking? Okay, Florida is really great-looking, with all those swaying palm trees and bright blue skies. But once we hit Camp Coral Reef it's going to be downhill all the way. Why? I'll tell you...

A few weeks ago Cheryl and I were in the school bookshop. Cheryl was looking for a travel book on Florida. I was just . . . looking.

But just as I was about to grab a book about ballet, I saw a big paperback called *The Worst That Can Happen.* I flipped through it and almost flipped myself.

Two of a Kind Diaries

The book tells you everything that can go wrong – any time, any place. Like there's a gross chapter on the stuff you can find in your chicken nuggets. And what can happen to your toenails after you go for a pedicure. (You don't want to know.)

But there was one chapter that really made my teeth curl. A chapter on water sports!

"Cheryl, check it out!" I called. "Did you know that jellyfish are practically invisible? That's why people step on them and get stung!"

Cheryl looked at the book and laughed. "Come on, Ashley," she said. "You can't go through life expecting the worst all the time."

"Bad things do happen, you know," I said.

Cheryl shrugged. "Then if someone tosses you a lemon, you have to make the best of it – make lemonade!" she declared.

"Lemonade," I said, flipping through the book. "I'll bet there's a chapter on lemons, too. And what happens when you swallow too many seeds—"

"Girlfriend, put that nasty book down!" Cheryl ordered.

But I had other plans.

Shore Thing

"I'm buying this book," I told Cheryl. "Maybe it's not too late to change Mary-Kate's mind about Camp Coral Reef."

"You're showing that book to your sister?" Cheryl asked. "Mary-Kate 'Fearless' Burke?"

"No way!" I said. "She'd just call me a wimp."

Instead I tried to talk Mary-Kate out of going to Florida and into going to New York City.

"New York?" Mary-Kate asked as we hung out in the student lounge. "Why New York?"

"Because I want to wake up in a city that never sleeps!" I exclaimed. "I want to see its treasures. The museums, the theatres—"

"The shops?" Mary-Kate joked.

"Hey," I said. "Can I help it if I'd rather try on clam diggers than dig for clams?"

It was no use. Mary-Kate was set on the Keys and I was set for *disaster!*

But later I found out that Ross Lambert was going to Camp Coral Reef, too. That's when I gave in. I mean, Ross and I probably won't see each other for the rest of the summer. And he's the only boy I've ever liked. Okay, okay, there've been more. Lots more. But not all of them liked me back!

111

Two of a Kind Diaries

In the end it was Dad in Chicago who made the decision. He thought the camp would be a "good educational experience." Spoken like a true college professor.

Whoops! Time out. One of the campers dropped an earring on the bus and everyone's looking for it. And guess what? It belongs to a boy!

I'm back. And my Coral Reef nightmare has already begun. Right now we're sitting outside the Main House while Mrs. Clare, our assistant headmistress, checks us in. Mrs. Clare is cool. She came on the trip with a supply of sun hats, sunscreen, and packets of oatmeal. I guess the White Oak tradition lives on, even in Florida.

When the bus pulled up to the camp half an hour ago we were all confused.

"This is a camp?" Jeremy asked. "Where are the bunks? And the mess hall? And the softball field?"

"This isn't that kind of camp, Jeremy," Mrs. Clare said. "We'll all be staying inside the beach house and studying at the Marine Centre down the road."

Mrs. Clare pointed out of the bus window. "In fact," she said, "there's the pool where you'll be learning how to scuba dive."

I stared at the pool. It looked cool and crystal clear and safe. I felt better until all the kids started

Shore Thing

pumping their fists in the air and chanting, "Scuba! Scuba! Scuba!"

That's when I felt really sick.

I mean, haven't they ever seen *Jaws*?

Chapter 2

Sunday

Hi, Diary!

Here it is. My first full day at Camp Coral Reef and all I can say is – this place rocks!

We spent most of the day getting to know each other (even though we already do!) and meeting the camp staff.

The director of the camp is a guy named Sid Pepper. Sid has long grey hair that he ties back in a ponytail. He wears white shorts and T-shirts with corny sayings like "Florida – the Funshine State." He also plays the guitar and sings about ships and whales. That's cool, because the only whale song I know is "Baby Beluga."

There's a counsellor for fishing and boating named Brad. A counsellor for photography named Keith. And a scuba instructor named Jenny. They all seem nice and their tans make Summer look pale.

And you should check out the big house we're all staying in. It has this huge porch that wraps all the way around. And all of the rooms have wicker furniture and fans on the ceiling.

"It's like something out of a 1930s movie!" Phoebe gasped. Just so you know, Diary, Phoebe

Shore Thing

likes vintage movies as much as she likes vintage clothes.

And you should see the dining room. It's nothing like the one back at White Oak.

"Where are the gargoyles?" Elise joked when we walked in. "And the paintings of the ex-headmistresses?"

Instead there are layers of fishing nets on the ceiling and wooden fish on the walls. And inside a big wicker cage are real, live parrots!

"Polly want a cracker?" Summer asked a parrot.

"Polly doesn't want a cracker," Jeremy said. "He wants a cheeseburger and fries. Trust me."

What I like best about Florida are all the palm trees. My favourites are the tall, skinny ones. Ashley likes the ones that look like cheerleader pom-poms. But the best is the beach at the back of our house. The sand is sugar-white and the Atlantic Ocean is the bluest blue I've ever seen. Is this paradise or what?

Too bad Ashley doesn't think so. After lugging our bags to our room I expected the usual argument – "Who gets the bed by the window?" So I was amazed when Ashley wanted the bed against the wall.

Two of a Kind Diaries

"You never know what exotic creatures might crawl through the window, Mary-Kate," Ashley said. "I read all about mosquitoes that carry malaria!"

"Malaria?" I asked. "Where'd you learn that?"

"Nowhere," Ashley said quickly. I caught her stuffing something deep into her backpack.

I held out my hand. "Let me see it. If we're going to share a room there'll be no secrets."

Ashley's shoulders dropped. She slowly pulled out a book and held it up.

"*The Worst That Can Happen*?" I cried.

Ashley told me all about the book. That's when I laughed out loud.

"It's not funny," Ashley said. "There's even a whole chapter on water sports. Like, did you know diving too deep could make your lungs explode? And your eyeballs pop?"

"But you won the swimming team medal three years ago," I told Ashley.

"Yeah," Ashley said. "But I wasn't being chased by a thirty-foot alligator!"

"Alligators stick to the swamps," I said. "Don't you remember that nature show on TV? Where that Australian guy actually

Shore Thing

wrestled the alligator with his bare hands?"

"You saw it," Ashley said. "I had my eyes closed!"

"What a wuss!" I laughed. "Maybe you *should* have gone to New York. The only alligators there are in shoe shops."

Ashley's eyes grew as big as Frisbees.

"A wuss?" she gasped. "I am not a wuss!"

"Are too," I said. "And thanks to that book, I'll bet you won't even make it through the next few weeks of camp. You'll be too scared to do anything!"

Ashley's face turned red. She folded her arms across her chest. "Oh, yeah?" she said. "Well, I bet that I can get through camp with flying colours! Not only that, I'm even going to pass my scuba test – the first time!"

"Oh, yeah?" I said. "Well, so am I. The bet is on!"

We hooked pinkies, which is what we always do when we make a bet. Then I told Ashley that the loser had to clean the winner's side of her dorm room at school. For six whole months!

"Not fair!" Ashley shrieked. "My side of my dorm room only needs a broom. Your side of your room needs a – bulldozer!"

Blah, blah, blah. Let her complain. All I can say

is, it'll be nice having maid service for a while! And my roomie Campbell will love having a clean room for a change!

Oh, well. Gotta run. There's a moonlight party on the beach tonight. I guess that means I don't need sunscreen!

Dear Diary,

My *Worst That Can Happen* book left out an important chapter – going on vacation with your twin sister!

Now I have to prove to Mary-Kate that I can survive the next two weeks without a hitch. That means fishing, boating, and worst of all – scuba diving!

"What was I *thinking*?" I asked myself all day.

Luckily there was a beach party at night to take my mind off the bet. While everyone else joined the limbo contest, I shared a beach blanket with Ross. We stared out at the ocean and talked.

"After camp ends I won't see you for two whole months," Ross said. "What are we going to do?"

Two months? The thought of not seeing Ross made my heart drop. But then I had an idea . . .

"I know!" I said. "You have a cousin who lives in Chicago. Why don't you visit him over the summer?"

Shore Thing

Ross's eyes lit up. He seemed to like the idea.

"I'll ask my mom and dad," he said. "If they say yes, then it's a go!"

I thought of something else.

"We can even go to the 4-You concert," I said. "They're playing in Chicago in August!"

In case I haven't told you, Diary, 4-You is our favourite singing group. They totally rule!

Ross smiled and gave me a high-five. I would have preferred a kiss but who's complaining?

Just then my cousin Jeremy walked over. His cheeks were puffed out like he was chewing on something.

"Do you like seafood?" Jeremy asked me through his full mouth.

"Seafood?" I said. "Sure."

Jeremy popped his mouth open to show me what was inside. "*See food!*" He laughed. "Get it?"

Ross laughed, but I was totally grossed. I grabbed a sponge football and tossed it at my cousin's head.

"Hey!" Jeremy complained.

"Nice pass!" a boy's voice said.

I spun round. Standing behind us was a boy of about thirteen. He had short brown hair and the lightest green eyes I ever saw.

"Ashley, this is Devon Benjamin," Ross said. "He's starting Harrington in September."

"Why weren't you on the plane or the bus with the rest of us?" I asked Devon.

"I hooked up with you guys today," Devon explained. "I live here in Florida. Over in Daytona Beach."

"You live by a beach?" I asked. "You must be a great swimmer."

"I—" Devon started to say.

"Devon practically has gills!" Jeremy interrupted. "He told me he's been scuba diving since he was ten!"

"Ten-and-a-half," Devon said.

"Scuba?" I gulped. I was having such a good time, I had almost forgotten about it.

The boys went off to join the limbo contest. I sat on the beach towel alone. But not for long.

"What's wrong, Ashley?" Mary-Kate asked as she sat down beside me. "Is there a chapter in your book about limbo?"

"Nope," I said coolly. "I just don't feel like play-

Shore Thing

ing right now." *The Worst That Can Happen* said you could break your back doing the limbo, but I wasn't going to mention that part to Mary-Kate.

"I can't wait until tomorrow," Mary-Kate said. She rubbed her hands. "It's our first day of activities. And last I looked, deep-sea fishing was on the schedule."

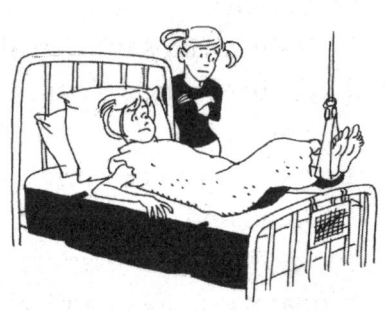

Deep-sea fishing? As in barracudas? Sharks? Seasickness? I tried not to let Mary-Kate see me shudder.

Instead I plastered on a big smile.

"Deep-sea fishing!" I cheered. "Bring it on!"

Just then I heard a loud yelp. I looked up and saw everyone running over to Seth Samuels.

"What happened?" I asked Cheryl.

"Seth just got stung by a big old jellyfish!" Cheryl said. "It was right under the limbo pole."

Diary, I've got to go. I have to finish reading up on jellyfish!

Chapter 3

Monday

Hey, Diary,

Ashley can say what she wants, but I love the Florida Keys.

This morning we had fresh fruit for breakfast. The last time I ate a papaya was back in Chicago and it was dried and rolled up. And I'll bet the ex-headmistresses from the 1800s never tasted pineapple-guava oatmeal.

But you have to be careful what you say around those parrots. I know because we picked the table right next to the parrot cage. Big mistake!

"You guys," Cheryl muttered over her pineapple juice. "Check out Mrs. Clare's sun hat!"

I glanced at the next table. Mrs. Clare's straw hat was the size of a manhole cover. It was so huge she had to tilt her head to get through the door.

"Too weird!" Elise snickered.

I heard a loud squawk. The red-and-green macaw named Taco began ruffling his feathers and rolling his head.

"Mrs. Clare!" he screeched. "Too weird! Arrk!"

Mrs. Clare glared at us from the next table.

"Thanks a lot, cracker breath!" Cheryl muttered to Taco.

Shore Thing

It was a good thing we had a big breakfast because this was our first day of activities.

First stop was the Marine Centre. I expected some little fish museum, but was I wrong. The big glass building with the whale sculpture in front has classrooms and laboratories – even an aquarium filled with live sea creatures. Keith pointed out fish I'd never heard of, like Harlequin Bass, Parrot Fish, and Nassau Groupers. There's a whole room filled with marine fossils and a six-foot giant squid hanging from the ceiling!

The squid may have been dead, but that didn't stop my sister from totally flipping out.

"Didn't you see?" Ashley cried to Keith. "He just waved at me! With his tentacles!"

"Don't tell me there's a chapter on the worst that can happen with a dead squid!" I joked.

"As a matter of fact there is," Ashley said. "A woman in Denver ate bad squid and was sick for weeks!"

Boy, Diary. Winning this bet is going to be even easier than I thought!

Two of a Kind Diaries

Dear Diary,

After we were totally freaked out by a giant dead squid, Brad took us fishing on the high seas. It wasn't very high, just enough to make most of us turn a pale shade of green from seasickness.

As Sid sailed the fishing boat out to sea, Brad made an announcement.

"Listen," he said. "We're not going to keep any of the fish we catch. We're going to throw them back into the sea. But first we're going to learn how to hook bait."

No problem, I thought. We'll probably use pieces of stale bread. Or those fuzzy little tackle things you see people fishing with.

Then all of a sudden Brad reached down and pulled out a small pail of worms! No, not the gummy type. These were the real things!

"We have sandworms and bloodworms," Brad told us. As if they were toppings in a frozen yogurt store.

"Or you can use these guys," Brad said. He reached into a tackle box and pulled out a jar of tiny dried-up fish. "They're not alive and it's a good thing because you have to hook them through their eyes."

Shore Thing

My mouth dropped open. I mean, did you ever hear of anything so yucky?

Luckily I wasn't the only grossed-out camper. Justin said he had 'worm-phobia.' Summer turned pale for the first time this year. Phoebe almost dropped her reporter pad and pencil overboard.

"Okay," Brad said. He picked up a worm between two fingers. "Who wants to go first?"

"Why don't you go, Ashley?" Jeremy called out.

"Me?" I asked. "Why me?"

Jeremy faced the other campers. "Because when Ashley was in kindergarten she found a tiny worm in the sandbox," he said. "And she totally freaked out!"

"Oh, I remember!" Mary-Kate said. "Ashley climbed to the top of the monkey bars and wouldn't come down for an hour!"

My cheeks burned as everyone laughed.

Now the whole camp thought I was a baby.

"Oh, Brad!" I called, raising my hand. "I'll go first!"

"Are you sure, Ashley?" Brad asked. "If you don't like worms—"

"Are you kidding?" I scoffed. "I eat worms like that for breakfast. Bring 'em on!"

I threw back my shoulders and marched over to

Brad. I expected him to hand me a worm. Instead he pointed to the pail and said, "Dig in!"

"Dig in?" I gulped. "O-o-okay."

I tried to blur my eyes as I kneeled by the pail. Then I played a little mind game.

These are not worms, I told myself as I reached in. These are yummy liquorice whips. Cherry liquorice whips...

It worked until I actually touched the worms. Cherry liquorice whips didn't squirm or wiggle!

"Excuse me?" I gulped. I wiped my hand off on my shorts. "I think I'll try the little fish instead. They're more of a ... challenge."

"Ha," I heard Jeremy snicker. "I knew it."

"Go for it," Brad said. He opened the jar and tossed me a tiny dried-up fish. "But aim straight for the eye."

I took the tiny fish between my fingers. Then Brad carefully handed me a hook.

Aim for the eye, I told myself as I brought the hook closer to the fish. "Aim for the eye..."

Then...

"Eeek!" Jeremy squeaked.

It was just a dumb joke. But I screamed and

Shore Thing

dropped the little fish on my leg. I jerked my leg – and knocked over the pail of worms. The worms took off across the deck.

I groaned as everyone ran to scoop them up. Then I sat down on a coil of rope and buried my face in my hands.

"Cheer up," a voice said. "You've made the worms very happy."

I looked up and saw Devon Benjamin smiling at me with those big green eyes.

"You think?" I asked.

"Sure," Devon said. "Wouldn't you rather be on deck than in the belly of some fish?"

Then Devon gave a little wave and joined the worm rescue.

What a nice guy, I thought. And so cute!

After Sid, Brad, and the campers scooped up most of the worms, all eyes turned to me.

"Wow!" I said with a nervous laugh. "Slippery little guys, aren't they?"

And, Diary, that was just the beginning! I'd tell you what happened when I went fishing, but the boys are outside slipping gummy worms under my door.

Not funny!

Two of a Kind Diaries

Dear Diary,

I'm back and writing to you from the porch this time. I don't want to write in my room with Ashley around, because this is going to be all about her.

Diary, Ashley's adventures in bait-hooking were bad enough. But when it came time to fish she went over the top. Literally!

After we got the hang of the fishing rods, Brad told us to drop our lines in the water. We all expected to get a bite right away. Instead we waited. And waited . . .

Then suddenly—

"I've got a bite!" Ashley cried out. From the way her fishing pole was bending, I could tell she wasn't kidding.

"Reel in the line!" Brad shouted.

"Okay!" Ashley said. She gritted her teeth as she tugged at the pole. "This fish is really big!"

We all ran over to help, but Ashley pushed us away.

"Stand back!" she cried. "I'm bringing this one in by myself!"

"Okay, Ashley," Brad called. "Reel it in as you

Shore Thing

step back slowly. And make sure you don't grip too hard."

We all watched as Ashley did exactly what Brad said.

"Maybe it's a barracuda," Elise said.

"Or a swordfish," Justin said.

"Nah," Jeremy said. "I'll bet it's a shark!"

"Shark?" Ashley cried.

Her pole jerked hard. Ashley held on – then screamed as she went flying over the rail – and into the ocean!

"Twin overboard!" Cheryl yelled. "Twin overboard!"

Everyone ran to the rail and looked over. We all wore life jackets, so Ashley didn't go under. But she probably wished she had.  Her face was red as a lobster from the embarrassment!

"Let that be a lesson, guys," Brad said after we pulled Ashley back in. "Never refuse help when reeling in a big fish."

Ashley gazed over the rail at her fishing pole floating out to sea in a ripple of currents.

Two of a Kind Diaries

"There it goes," she said. "My catch of the day."

"Oh, well," I said. "If it was a shark, you wouldn't want it anyway."

Ashley sighed and walked away.

I was going to remind her about our bet, but I changed my mind. She looked too upset. And I have to give her credit for trying.

That's it for now, Diary. Mrs. Clare just clued us in on a marshmallow roast on the beach. A marshmallow roast! I guess this is more like regular camp than I thought. See ya!

Chapter 4

Tuesday

Dear Diary,

The moment I woke up I knew it was the first day of scuba instruction. Probably because I had nightmares about it all night!

By the time I went down for breakfast I couldn't eat a thing. My stomach was already full – with butterflies!

"After breakfast we'll meet at the pool, where you'll suit up and get your scuba equipment," Jenny said. "We'll have our first classroom instruction later in the day."

"Scuba! Scuba! Scuba!" everyone yelled.

I yelled too just so Mary-Kate would think I was psyched.

When we filed into the pool area, Jenny handed out diving suits.

"Oh, none for me," Phoebe said. "I'm Phoebe Cahill. And I'm here to write my article for the *White Oak Acorn*."

Jenny looked confused. She looked at her list of students. "It says here that you're scheduled for scuba diving," she said. "All campers must participate."

Two of a Kind Diaries

Phoebe's eyes popped open behind her green-rimmed glasses. She clutched her reporter pad and pencil tightly.

"What?" Phoebe cried. "But I'm not cut out for sports! I'm more the intellectual type."

"Then you'll do great on the written test!" Jenny said with a smile. "And you can write all about your adventures in scuba for the paper."

"Phoebe! Phoebe! Phoebe!" everyone cheered.

Phoebe groaned and grabbed her diving suit. I knew exactly how she felt.

We put on our suits in the dressing rooms. They were tight and black and slick.

I looked around for Ross, but my eyes landed on Devon. He wasn't making seal noises like all the other boys. He looked calm and cool in his diving suit. And still very cute.

I gave my head a shake. What was I thinking? Ross was my boyfriend – and he was standing only a few feet away!

"Look!" Elise interrupted my thoughts. "That must be the equipment."

Shore Thing

I looked to see where Elise was pointing. There were racks and racks of tubes, belts, and masks.

"That's not scuba gear," Phoebe cried. "Those are instruments of torture!"

Jenny clapped her hands for attention.

"Listen up," she called out. "I want you all to see how a diver looks when he's ready to jump into the ocean."

The door to the boys' dressing room swung open. We all laughed as Jeremy stepped out in full scuba gear.

"Here's Jeremy modelling the equipment you'll need for your first dive," Jenny said.

Jeremy pretended to twirl like a supermodel.

"You'll all get a tank of compressed air," Jenny began. "A second-stage regulator and mouthpiece, a face mask, two submersible gauges – one to measure depth, the other to see how much air you have left in your tank—"

You mean it could run out? I thought.

"You'll also wear a weight belt to help you stay under," Jenny went on. "And fins on your feet to help propel you underwater."

Jeremy held up one foot and fell over.

"You're already wearing your wet suits. They help prevent hypothermia," Jenny said as Jeremy stood up. "Hypothermia is when your body temperature drops drastically."

"Are we diving in the Arctic?" Cheryl joked.

"No," Jenny said. "But the wet suit will also prevent cuts and scrapes underwater."

I gulped hard. Too much information!

"With the basic equipment a qualified diver can safely remain underwater for anywhere from a few minutes to two hours," Jenny said. "Any questions?"

I was dying to ask if my eyes would pop, but I didn't.

As Jenny passed out the masks, she mentioned all the great stuff we'd find under the sea once we had our certificates – bright pink coral, neon-coloured fish, and underwater plants. We would even borrow underwater cameras to take pictures.

"First we'll fit ourselves with the masks," Jenny said. "Just to get the feeling."

My heart raced as I struggled with the mask. I couldn't even get it over

Shore Thing

my head. Ross saw me panic and came over. He helped me adjust the straps and buckles. Soon the mask fit perfectly.

"All systems go!" Ross said.

I smiled under my mask and gave him a thumbs-up sign. My mask was on, and I didn't even freak.

A small step for scuba diving – a giant step for Ashley Burke!

I can't believe it, Diary. Maybe scuba diving won't be so bad after all.

And maybe I might even win this bet!

Dear Diary,

I thought I knew myself.

I like Rocky Road ice cream, the Chicago Cubs, and acting in school plays. I'm also good at sports.

At least until today . . .

"Here's your mask, Mary-Kate," Jenny said. "Now don't forget to adjust the buckle and straps. And make sure it's airtight."

"No problem," I said coolly. After all, I was the bathtub bubble-blowing champ of Chicago!

I stood next to Phoebe as we both adjusted our masks. Phoebe had hers on first.

"I can't breathe!" Phoebe gasped. She pointed to

her nose behind the scuba mask. "I can't breathe!"

"Breathe through your mouth," I told her.

"Oh," Phoebe said, taking a deep breath.

My mask adjusted, I pulled it over my face. For one second everything was fine.

Then something began to happen. It was as if the mask was closing in on me. Strangling me. Smothering me!

I ripped the mask off my face and took a deep breath.

"Mary-Kate, what's wrong?" Jenny asked.

"Nothing!" I gasped.

Jenny smiled. "It's okay to feel claustrophobic in your mask the first time," she said. "Lots of people do."

"I just had to sneeze," I said quickly. "And who wants to sneeze inside a scuba mask? Too gross!"

As Jenny walked away I glanced at Ashley. She was wearing her mask and looking totally cool.

Something was wrong with this picture. Ashley was the one who was supposed to be flipping out – not me!

Luckily class was over right after the masks. We changed into our regular clothes and headed back to our rooms for a midday break.

Ashley stuck around with Ross. I could see her

Shore Thing

chattering on and on about our "awesome" scuba lesson.

I went into my room and plopped down on my bed. I closed my eyes and took a deep breath.

The next time you put on a mask, you'll be fine, I told myself. There's nothing scary about scuba diving—

Knock! Knock!

I opened the door and saw Phoebe.

"Mary-Kate!" Phoebe said. "Where's Ashley? I need to talk to her!"

"She's with Ross," I said. "What's up?"

Phoebe walked past me and sat on Ashley's bed. She shook her head.

"It's my article!" she said. "How can I write about scuba diving when all I can think of is two weeks of physical torture?"

"You'll get the hang of it," I said.

"How can I?" Phoebe cried. "The closest I've ever come to going underwater was looking in the fish tank in my dentist's office."

I sat down next to Phoebe. Then suddenly—

"Ow!" I said. Something hard was tucked under Ashley's blanket.

I pulled it out. It was Ashley's book, *The Worst That Can Happen*. "It's that dumb book!" I groaned.

"What book?" Phoebe asked. She picked it up and read the title. Then she began to flip through it.

"Wow," Phoebe said. "Did you know that building a snowman can freeze your hands?"

She kept flipping through the pages.

"Oh, no," Phoebe said. "There's a whole chapter on scuba diving. Did you know you could get something called compression sickness? Air embolism? Physical exhaustion?"

I blinked. Somehow the book didn't seem so funny anymore.

"What else?" I gulped.

"Injuries from marine life—" Phoebe gulped.

"Next chapter!" I urged.

Phoebe turned the page. Her jaw dropped.

"Mary-Kate!" she said. "Did you know that baby alligators can swim up through drains? And toilets?"

"I don't think I want to hear any more," I said. We both jumped when we heard Ashley out in the hall.

Shore Thing

"Don't tell Ashley we were reading her book," I begged Phoebe. "I don't want her to know that I got scared."

"I promise," Phoebe said. "But it's okay to be scared, Mary-Kate."

That was easy for her to say. She doesn't have a major bet to win!

Chapter 5

Wednesday

Hi, Diary!

When I woke up this morning I was actually looking forward to our next scuba lesson. Imagine that!

Today we wore our bathing suits and got to try out our compressed air tanks. Mine wasn't as heavy as I thought it would be. And I had no trouble breathing under the shallow water of the pool.

"And now for a surprise," Jenny said after we practised breathing. "We're going to play a game of dive and retrieve."

Jenny explained that we would be split up into teams of two. Then we would dive into the pool and pick up colourful weights under the water.

"Our first team will be Summer and Justin," Jenny called out. "Our second team will be Seth and Cheryl..."

I glanced over at Mary-Kate. I know she's my twin, but I didn't want to team up with her. She would only show off and remind me about our bet!

"I hope they team us up," Ross whispered to me.

"Me, too!" I said.

"Our third team will be Ashley and Devon!" Jenny called out.

Shore Thing

Devon. Not Ross. I know I should have felt a little bad about it, but teaming up with Devon was going to be fun. I just knew it.

Jenny dropped the first weight in the pool. Then she signaled for Summer and Justin to dive. Everyone cheered as they swam underwater to search for it.

"This is cool," Devon said to me.

I glanced at Devon. He was looking at me through his long, silky black eyelashes.

"Yeah," I said slowly. "Way cool."

As we waited for our turn, Devon told me all about his adventures in scuba. He'd even gone diving in Hawaii!

"What was the neatest thing you ever saw under the sea?" I asked Devon.

"Once I saw something shiny on the sea floor," Devon explained. "It turned out to be an ancient Spanish coin."

"Wow!" I said.

Cheryl and Seth swam up with the bright blue weight. Then it was our turn.

"I might not be too good at this," I told Devon as we walked to the pool.

"You'll be great," Devon said. "Stick with me."

Two of a Kind Diaries

Jenny gave us the signal, and we dived into the pool. The weight belt around my waist helped me to stay under. I tried to keep calm as I breathed through my mouthpiece.

Devon pointed to the blue weight. We flapped our flippers and swam towards the weight. Our hands touched as we reached for it at the same time.

That's when it happened. My heart began to flutter and my head felt like it was in the clouds.

No – it wasn't decompression sickness. It was the same feeling I had when I first met Ross Lambert!

The next thing I felt was a pang of guilt. I mean – what if I'm actually falling for another boy?

Dear Diary,

I could sure use a dish of Rocky Road ice cream today. No. Make that a whole container!

When I found out we'd have our second scuba class today, my stomach did a triple flip. Would I totally choke like yesterday? And if I did – would Ashley notice?

Standing next to Phoebe didn't help either.

"I heard we're diving in the pool today!" Phoebe

Shore Thing

whispered. "Do you remember what Ashley's book said about diving?"

I didn't want to hear about it again. I put my mask on, and this time I managed to keep it on. I also did pretty well with my oxygen tank. Until I had a horrible thought . . .

"Hey, Phoebe," I whispered. "What happens if you fall backwards on the tank?"

"Forget that," Phoebe whispered back. "What happens if these tanks explode?"

Explode? That did it!

"Jenny?" I blurted. "I can't finish the class today!"

"Why not, Mary-Kate?" Jenny asked.

"My stomach!" I said, grabbing my middle. "It must have been that kiwi oatmeal I had this morning!"

Jenny looked concerned. "Then you'd better go back to your room," she said. "But have someone walk you back."

Ashley raised her hand. "I'll go with her," she said.

"No!" Phoebe shouted. "I will! I will! I will!"

Phoebe and I dashed out of the pool area. We

leaned against the fence and sighed with relief.

"Good thinking, Mary-Kate," Phoebe said. "You got us *both* out of this class!"

But I was still worried. I mean, how could I go from being super-jock to super-chicken in just a few days?

Diary, help!

Chapter 6

Thursday

Dear Diary,
My drama class training is really paying off. This morning everyone believed me when I said I was still sick.

Everyone except Ashley.

"So how are you really feeling, Mary-Kate?" Ashley asked. She tilted her head as she watched me in bed.

"Awwwwwful!" I moaned. "My head is stuffed, my nose is running, and my head is pounding!"

"That's weird," Ashley said. "Yesterday you told Jenny that your stomach hurt."

"My stomach hurts too!" I blurted. "The pain's just moving up, that's all!"

Ashley sighed. She pulled a shirt over her bathing suit and headed to the door.

"Well, you'll be missing our third scuba class," she said. "And there's only three more until the certification test."

As if I didn't know!

"Anyhow I'll look in on you later," Ashley went on. "After scuba class. After I blow everybody away with my incredible diving skills!"

I rolled my eyes. Ashley was busting my chops about the bet. And she still didn't know how scared I was!

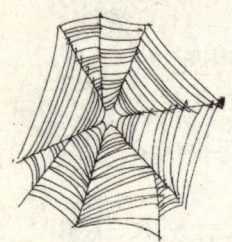

The door closed and I was alone. I stared up at the ceiling and noticed a small spider's web.

Spiders, I thought. I grabbed Ashley's book and opened to the chapter on spiders.

"'A bite from a tarantula can cause instant death,'" I read to myself. "Death?"

I ran for the door. I was about to call for help when I stopped short.

"I've got to get a grip," I told myself. "Especially if I'm going to win this bet!"

But first I had to deal with a serious case of scuba-phobia!

"I know!" I told myself. "I'll practise blowing bubbles in the bathtub. If I could do it when I was five, I can do it now!"

I changed into my bathing suit. Then I grabbed the mask and carried it to the girls' shower room. Next to the two shower cubicles was a white bathtub with iron legs. I turned on the cool water and filled it up.

"Okay," I said, stepping into the tub. "Here goes."

Shore Thing

I slipped the mask over my face. I tried not to panic as I dunked under the water.

Cool, I thought as I peered through my scuba mask. I could see every tiny crack in the porcelain. Even the silver drain seemed to sparkle.

I began to relax and blow bubbles. Until I remembered what Phoebe said about bathtub drains . . .

Alligators! I thought. Baby alligators swim up through drains and toilets!

"Ahhh!" I jumped up and pulled off my mask.

A knock on the door made me jump.

"Is somebody in there?" Mrs. Clare called.

"No, Mrs. Clare," I called back. "Nobody here but us chickens!"

Dear Diary,

Call the newspaper because I did it! Today I won a contest of underwater steal the bacon!

"You see?" Devon told me after instruction. "You never know what you can do until you try!"

I knew I liked Devon Benjamin. And I wanted to hang out with him – but how could I? Especially

147

Two of a Kind Diaries

since Ross and I had planned to spend lots of time together. And Ross was my boyfriend . . .

"Sid said he'd drive a group of us to town after lunch," Ross said. "How about it?"

"Sure!" I said.

I was hoping Devon would sign up for the trip, but he didn't. Instead it was just Ross, Elise, Justin, and me.

When we reached the town it turned out to be only three blocks long. There were small shops and huts selling boating tours, seafood, and souvenirs.

Ross and I went inside this cool shop that sold sunglasses, postcards, stuffed toy alligators, and loads of T-shirts. But while Ross looked at ships in bottles, I was on the lookout for Devon Benjamin.

Maybe he borrowed the camp bike and rode to town. Maybe he had to buy a present for his mother. Or maybe for his sister, if he has one. Naturally he doesn't have a girlfriend! He couldn't! He wouldn't! Don't even go there!

But just as I was about to buy some saltwater taffy, I saw something awesome dangling in front of my eyes!

It was a beautiful coral choker!

I spun around and saw Ross. He was holding the pink-and-white necklace and grinning.

Shore Thing

"For me?" I asked.

Ross nodded with a big smile on his face.

"Put it on," he urged.

From Ross!

I walked over to a mirror framed with shells. I hooked the choker around my neck. It looked great. But deep inside I felt awful. How could I accept a gift from Ross when just a few minutes ago I was hoping that Devon would show up?

"Thanks, Ross," was all I could say. "It's beautiful."

Oh, Diary! Why does Devon have to be so cute?

Chapter 7

Friday

Dear Diary,

I decided I am not going to let my fears spoil my fun. So this morning when we had our photography work-  shop, I turned my attention to the art of capturing wildlife. Besides, what could be dangerous about taking pictures?

Keith showed us slides of birds and tropical fish. The colours were incredibly bright and beautiful.

But then a slide appeared of a snake curled up on a rock.

"You got that from a magazine, right?" Summer asked. "Like *National Geometric*?"

"*National Geographic*, Summer!" Cheryl groaned.

"No way!" Keith said. "One of the campers from last year snapped this shot. Right near the swamp."

"Aren't most snakes – poisonous?" I asked.

"Some of them are," Keith said. "You'll learn all about them in marine biology."

I nodded. Then I felt Phoebe tap my shoulder.

"Remember to check out the chapter on snakes later!" she whispered.

Anyway, Diary, I've got to fly. Camp Coral Reef is throwing us a pizza party tonight in the rec room.

Shore Thing

Sure, I'm still worried about scuba diving. But extra cheese and pepperoni always makes things easier.

Ciao!

Dear Diary,

We just had the most awesome pizza party and I am stuffed to the gills! (That's a Florida Keys fish joke. Everyone's saying it.)

My favourite cheese and mushroom pie was there. But I had to be convinced that the droopy green stuff on one was spinach – not seaweed!

When the local DJ played a slow song, I danced with Ross. A few months ago I would have been floating on the moon, but tonight I felt totally guilty. The coral necklace Ross gave me seemed to make me itch.

Diary, is there a way for a boy to know that you MIGHT like someone else? Do your eyes twitch? Do you smell weird? Do you eat your pizza differently? I sure hope not!

The slow song ended and Ross and I walked over to the chips and dip. As I chewed on a chip with guacamole I looked around the room. No Devon.

"Want some pineapple punch, Ashley?" Ross asked.

"Sure," I said. He walked over to the drinks table and I wandered over to the window. I looked out and saw the moon glimmering on the ocean.

I slipped out of the back door on to the porch. Guess who was there leaning against a rail – Devon!

"Hi," I said, trying to ignore my racing heart.

Devon looked back and smiled. "Hey!"

I leaned over the rail next to him. Not too close.

"Great party!" I said.

"It would be better if they didn't play so much 4-You!" Devon groaned.

I was hoping I heard wrong. 4-You is my favourite band.

"What's wrong with 4-You?" I asked.

Devon shrugged. "They sound like they're in pain," he said.

I wanted to argue but didn't. So Devon doesn't like 4-You. Well, nobody's perfect!

"We're going canoeing tomorrow," Devon said. "I saw it on the schedule."

"I've never gone canoeing," I said. "What's it like?"

"It's great!" Devon said. "Maybe we can share a canoe, and I'll show you the ropes."

Shore Thing

Share a canoe? I was so excited I couldn't speak. I pictured myself in a canoe with Devon. Gliding over crystal clear water under the bright Florida stars—

"Ashley?" Ross's voice interrupted my thoughts.

"Huh?" I spun around. Ross was standing at the back door. He was holding two cups of pineapple punch.

"Oh, hi, Ross!" I said. I hurried to him and pulled him back into the rec room.

"I couldn't find you," he said. "Let's finish this punch and dance again. They're playing some more 4-You!"

"Great!" I said.

I had a feeling Ross didn't suspect anything. But that only made me feel guiltier!

Chapter 8

Saturday

Dear Diary,

Today at breakfast I sat between Mary-Kate and Ross. Out of the corner of my eye I saw Devon eating a corn muffin with guava jelly. Did he remember what he had said about the canoe trip today? I hoped so!

"Think of this canoe trip as practice," Brad said after breakfast. "For the race in a few days!"

"Race?" Excited whispers filled the dining room.

"I'll explain the race later," Brad said. "Are there any questions about today's trip?"

"Where are we going to canoe?" I asked. Down a crystal clear stream? A quiet lake? A babbling brook?

"The swamp!" Brad answered with a smile. "Where else are you going to see tropical trees, birds, and insects?"

Insects? I was hoping Mary-Kate didn't see the big lump in my throat!

Mrs. Clare instructed us to pack our backpacks with sandwiches, juice, and bug lotion. Then we filed into the camp minibus where I sat next to Mary-Kate.

"I am so totally psyched," Mary-Kate said. "I

Shore Thing

hope we do see some alligators. Lots of them!"

"Well, I hope we see snakes," I said. "A big mamba!"

"What's that?" Mary-Kate asked.

"Something poisonous," I said. "I read about it in my *Worst That Can Happen* book. Chapter five."

"Nuh-uh!" Mary-Kate said, shaking her head. "Snakes are in chapter seven—" She bit her lip.

I was about to ask her how she knew that when Brad stopped the bus. We filed out and saw canoes and oars lined up on the muddy bank of the swamp.

We stood and stared at the brownish green water. Sticking out of the muck were swamp grass and gnarly tree branches that looked like claws. Curtains of moss dripped from trees like dark green slime.

"I think I saw this in a movie," Jeremy said.

"*The African Queen*?" Phoebe asked.

"No," Jeremy said. "*The Creature from the Black Lagoon*!"

"Okay, gang!" Brad called. He clapped his hands. "Grab your backpacks and team up in groups of three!"

Two of a Kind Diaries

Phoebe grabbed Mary-Kate's arm. Mary-Kate grabbed Elise.

"So are we a team or what?" a voice asked.

I turned and saw Devon grinning at me.

"You bet!" I said, smiling back. But then I saw Ross walking toward us. "You, me – and Ross Lambert!"

Brad gave us a canoeing demonstration. We practised holding our oars. Then we dragged our canoes into the swamp. Bullfrogs boomed from nearby islands and branches.

"Smooth sailing all the way!" Devon said. He took hold of the canoe and jumped in the back.

Ross looked disappointed. I think *he* wanted to steer. Instead he took the front and I took the middle.

Paddling our canoe down the swamp was like pushing through thick, sticky oatmeal. But as Devon pointed out pelicans, horseshoe crabs, and a few deer on the bank, the swamp began to look less scary and more exciting!

"The roots growing out of the water are called mangroves," Devon explained. "We have to be careful not to get stuck in one."

"Hey!" Ross called out. "What's that?"

I turned. Ross was pointing to a huge turtle sitting on a nearby island.

Shore Thing

The turtle blinked at us as we steered closer to the island. He was about the size of Mary-Kate's basketball.

"Watch this," Ross said. He leaned out of the canoe and hoisted the turtle into the boat.

"What are you doing?" I cried.

"Taking him back to camp," Ross said. "I want to show the guys what we found."

"You better put him back, Ross," Devon warned. "Turtles can be dangerous."

Ross didn't listen. He placed the turtle on the floor of our canoe – right in front of me!

"Here, Ashley!" Ross laughed. "A souvenir!"

As I began to slide away from it, the turtle thrust his head out and grabbed hold of my trainer with his mouth!

"Ahhh!" I shouted. "Get him off meeee!" I shrieked, shaking my foot.

Ross pulled at the turtle. He even tapped on his shell. But that turtle didn't budge!

"Watch out!" Devon warned. He reached out and grabbed my ankle. With a swift jerk he yanked the trainer off my foot!

Carefully Devon pried the turtle's jaw from my

Two of a Kind Diaries

trainer. Then he placed the turtle back into the swamp.

"A snapping turtle," Ross said, shrugging. "Who knew?"

I was so grateful I leaned over and gave Devon a big hug. Big mistake!

Dear Diary,

I may be snug in my bed now but just hours ago I was in the middle of a mucky, yucky swamp!

The minute Phoebe, Elise, and I stepped into our canoe I knew there'd be trouble. . .

"Stop shaking the canoe!" Elise demanded.

"How can I stop shaking the canoe when I can't stop shaking myself?" Phoebe cried.

Phoebe was dressed in vintage army camouflage.

She wore a 1940s hat on her head with a net to cover her face.

"No way am I getting a mosquito bite," Phoebe told us. "I read all about malaria in that book."

"What book?" Elise asked.

I spun around and glared at Phoebe.

"Um – *Little Women*!" Phoebe said quickly.

"They get malaria?" Elise cried.

Shore Thing

"No!" Phoebe said. "I mean yes. In the sequel!"

Our canoe drifted through swamp grass and soupy water. I sat in the bow of the canoe, which meant I saw everything first. Every bug. Every snake. Every horseshoe crab.

The swamp got narrower as we paddled. "This hanging moss is gross!" I said, brushing it aside. "And what's that glittery stuff coming up?"

"Glittery?" Elise gasped. "Where?"

Elise loved anything glittery. But as we got closer, I was pretty sure she wouldn't love this.

I gasped as layers and layers of spiders' webs stretched over our heads. With big yellow and black spiders!

"Ahhggggh!" Phoebe cried.

We ducked, but it was no use. The spiders' webs seemed to dip lower and lower. They practically brushed our heads!

"Little Miss Muffet was right," I shouted. "I'm out of here!"

"Where are you going?" Phoebe demanded.

I looked around. There was a tiny, mossy island about fifteen feet away.

"There!" I said.

"I'm right behind you!" Phoebe declared.

Phoebe and I swung our legs over the canoe.

"Stop!" Elise shouted. "You can't swim in the swamp!"

"Why not?" I asked.

"Hel-lo?" Elise asked. "Haven't you ever heard of alligators?"

Phoebe and I both froze.

"Alligators?" we shouted at the same time.

We swung our legs back into the canoe.

"Now get a grip, will you?" Elise demanded.

I gritted my teeth as we paddled on. The spiders' webs began to thin out. And we made it safely to the other side.

And not a moment too soon.

Later on the bus, Ashley asked me how the ride went.

I was dying to tell Ashley the truth. That I wasn't as brave as I said. That I was probably a bigger wimp than she was. And that I wish I never, ever made that stupid bet.

But I didn't.

"Great!" I told her. "Can't wait for that race!"

Now Ashley is busy brushing her teeth, so I'm going to check out her *The Worst That Can Happen* book.

I want to see what it says about mosquito bites.

And malaria!

Chapter 9

Sunday

Dear Diary,

You are not going to believe what happened today.

I spent all night scratching these mosquito bites I got in the swamp yesterday. So the minute the sun came up, I reached for Ashley's book. I flipped through it quietly under the covers.

"Malaria," I said. "What does it say about malaria?"

I found malaria in the book and read to myself. Phoebe was right. Malaria *was* carried by mosquitoes!

"The symptoms of malaria are severe headaches, chills, and extremely high fever . . ."

My head began to ache. I broke out into a cold sweat. And from what I saw – my skin was pretty red!

"Mary-Kate – what are you doing?" Ashley's voice demanded.

I gasped and popped my head out of the covers.

"I don't feel good," I blurted out.

"What do you have now?" Ashley asked.

"Malaria!" I shrieked.

"What?" Ashley cried. She ran over to my bed and felt my head. "You *are* kind of warm."

"I knew it!" I groaned. "It's been nice knowing you, Ashley. You can have my 4-You CDs. And give my Chicago Cubs jerseys to my roommate, Campbell! And tell Dad—"

"Mary-Kate!" Ashley said. "You might just have a cold. What makes you think it's malaria?"

"Because," I said, shoving Ashley's book deeper under the covers, "the mosquitoes in that swamp were the size of turkeys!"

"Okay," Ashley said. She began to look concerned. "I'll tell the counsellors. Maybe they can get the camp doctor to come here."

Big ugly Mosquito

Ashley pulled on a pair of shorts and a T-shirt. She was about to leave when she turned towards the night table.

"Did you see my book?" she asked. "It was on the night table last night."

"Your book?" I asked. "Um. No. I didn't see it."

Ashley shook her head and left. I lay in bed during breakfast and stared at the ceiling.

Maybe having malaria won't be so bad, I thought. I would get lots of attention. And I wouldn't have to do any more camp activities.

Shore Thing

I wouldn't even have to take the scuba certification test—

A knock on the door interrupted my thoughts.

"Come in," I called.

A woman with dark hair opened my door. "Hello, Mary-Kate," she said with a smile. "I'm Dr. Alvarez. I heard you're not feeling too well."

"Yes," I answered.

The doctor listened to my chest and popped a thermometer in my mouth. Then she examined my arms and legs. After all that she smiled again.

"You can tell me, Dr. Alvarez," I said. "I'm tough. At least I used to be."

"Tell you what?" Dr. Alvarez asked.

I took a deep breath. "That I have malaria!"

The doctor began to laugh.

"I'm sorry!" Dr. Alvarez said. "It's just that there is no malaria in Florida. You'd have to go all the way to Africa to catch that."

I plopped my head back on the pillow. I was never so relieved – and embarrassed – in my life.

"You do have a pretty bad sunburn, though," Dr. Alvarez said. "I recommend cold compresses and calamine lotion. Stay inside today. And use lots and lots of sunscreen tomorrow!"

The doctor gave me a pink bottle of calamine

lotion. Then I thanked her, and she left.

"Now there's only one more thing I have to do to feel better," I said to myself as I jumped out of bed. I reached under the covers and pulled out *The Worst That Can Happen*.

"I have to stop reading this stupid book!"

Dear Diary,

Good news. Mary-Kate does not have malaria!

"I'm glad you're okay," I told Mary-Kate when I checked up on her before scuba class.

"Me, too," Mary-Kate said. "But the doctor wants me to stay out of the sun today. I'm just so upset that I have to miss scuba."

I looked at Mary-Kate with that big grin on her face. She didn't look very upset to me.

"Well, you can't keep missing scuba diving," I said. "We're going to take our scuba certification test in four days. Remember our bet?"

"Don't worry!" Mary-Kate shrugged. "The bet's still on – and I'm going to win."

I tried to stay away from Devon today. After that snapping turtle incident yesterday, I have a hunch Ross knows I like him. At breakfast this morning, Ross barely took his nose out of his oatmeal.

Shore Thing

"What's the matter?" I asked.

"You didn't have to hug him," he muttered, glaring at Devon across the room.

"That was just a friendly hug," I insisted. "It didn't mean anything."

But I don't think Ross believed me.

"This afternoon there'll be a choice of activities," Sid announced during lunch. "You can either take a photography workshop on the beach or see a film on sharks at the marine biology centre."

Sid asked for a show of hands. I watched Devon raise his hand for photography. Then I saw Ross raise his hand for the shark film.

"Ashley," Sid said. "You have to choose an activity."

My head was spinning. The last thing I wanted to see was a film about sharks. But if I chose photography, Ross would think I just wanted to hang out with Devon.

"What will it be, Ashley?" Sid asked.

"Mary-Kate!" I blurted. "I mean, my sister is stuck in her room today. I want to keep her company."

"Well, that's nice of you, Ashley," Sid said.

Diary, what else could I do?

So when everybody went off to their activities, I headed upstairs to our room.

Two of a Kind Diaries

"Mary-Kate?" I called softly as I opened the door. No answer. Mary-Kate was fast asleep.

I sat on the wicker chair and glanced out of the window. The beach looked so inviting. Maybe I'd just take a little walk. No use wasting the sun, I thought.

I glanced back over at Mary-Kate, who was still in la-la land. Then I decided to go out.

And guess who I ran into on the beach. Keith and the photography workshop!

Keith had no problem with me joining in. He gave me a camera and told me that the pictures I took would develop before my eyes in just seconds. After a quick lesson on loading film we began snapping away.

Elise looked for starfish. Jeremy was on the hunt for giant water bugs. (Yuck!) And for a moment I forgot about Devon and searched the beach for exotic wildlife.

"Ew!" I said. I pointed to something scurrying across the sand. "What's that thing?"

"It's a sand crab!" Keith said with a grin. "And he'd make a great shot. Don't you think?"

I ran after it and snapped a picture.

Shore Thing

Keith was right. Everything looked great through a camera lens. Even something with a million legs!

I was having a great time taking pictures of tropical flowers, pelicans – even an awesome white cockatoo up in a tree. Until I spotted the most beautiful creature of all – Devon Benjamin!

Sure, we talked a bit. And he hung around while I took wildlife photos.

So can I help it if Devon just happens to be in the background?

Dear Diary,

I know I already wrote to you today, Diary, but have I got news about Ashley!

After a nice snooze I was eating a late lunch in the dining room. My sunburn had faded a bit and didn't hurt so much. And I was feeling braver after throwing out that stupid book!

"I am going to ace that scuba test," I told myself.

"Scuba! Scuba!" Taco squawked. His cage was behind me but I knew he had his eye on the cracker in my conch chowder!

"There you are, Mary-Kate!" Ashley said as she rushed into the dining room. She was holding something in her hands and looking very excited.

"Where were you?" I asked my sister.

"Wildlife photography!" Ashley announced. She smiled as she laid her pictures out on the table.

I studied the shots. The first few were of this crabby looking critter. The rest were a little more – human!

"Half of these pictures are of Devon!" I exclaimed.

Ashley's eyes opened wide. "Devon who?" she blurted.

"Devon Benjamin!" I said. I pointed to the pictures one by one. "Devon waving from a sand dune. Devon taking a picture of a cockatoo. Devon sticking his foot in the ocean and pretending he's cold. Devon, Devon, Devon!"

"Shhh!" Ashley hissed, grabbing my arm.

"Ow!" I cried. "Sunburn!"

"Sorry!" Ashley said. "But all those pictures of Devon are just a coincidence."

"I don't think so," I said. "I can tell you like him because you got that look on your face when you laid out his pictures," I said.

"Look?" Ashley demanded. "What look?"

"The faraway look you always have when you're in love," I said. "Like you're looking at a sunset!"

Shore Thing

Ashley's shoulders dropped. Call it a twin thing but I knew she was about to come clean.

"Okay!" Ashley cried. "I do have a crush on Devon. But whatever you do, you have to promise not to tell Ross!"

"I promise," I said. Then I smiled and began to sing softly. "Ashley loves Devon. Ashley loves Devon."

"Mary-Kate!" Ashley complained. She bit into one of my rolls. "By the way, Mary-Kate. Did you notice that I'm acing all of the camp activities?"

"That's nice," I said.

"Which reminds me," Ashley said slowly. "This is the fourth scuba class you missed today. And yesterday after the canoe trip your knees were shaking so much you could barely get out of the canoe. What was that all about?"

"So I was suffering from seasickness!" I blurted.

"Whatever," Ashley said. She began to collect her pictures. "I'm bringing these back to my room. And remember when you see Ross, don't tell him I spent the day with Devon. He thinks I was keeping you company."

Aha! Now I know Ashley's little secret.

And if I'm not more careful – she's going to find out mine!

Chapter 10

Monday

Dear Diary,

The most awful thing happened at breakfast this morning. And it's all Mary-Kate's fault!

"Hey, everybody!" Jeremy called when Mary-Kate and I came down for breakfast. "Ashley has a new boyfriend!"

I felt my legs stiffen.

"What are you talking about?" I demanded.

"As if you didn't know!" Summer giggled.

"Ashley loves Devon, Ashley loves Devon," Jeremy began to sing.

"Ashley loves Devon!" Taco screeched. "Arrrk!"

The table began to snicker. Ross's mouth was a thin grim line as he looked at me from the corner of his eye.

"Devon is a hottie! Devon is a hottie!" Taco screeched. "Arrk!"

"I taught him how to say that!" Jeremy laughed.

I pulled Mary-Kate aside. "I told you not to tell!"

"I didn't!" Mary-Kate insisted.

"Then who did?" I snapped. "We were the only ones in the dining room when I told you!"

Shore Thing

"I don't have a clue!" Mary-Kate shrugged.

"Yeah, sure," I snapped. I was going to sit down next to Ross but he was already leaving the dining room.

"Ross, wait up!" I said out in the hall.

Ross spun around. "Doesn't that necklace mean anything to you?" he asked.

"Yes!" I said, touching the coral choker. "You know how much I like you, Ross."

What I didn't say was that I liked Devon, too. But I didn't have a chance. Ross turned and walked away.

It's not fair, Diary! A person can like two flavours of ice cream – even three – and get away with it. So why can't I like two boys?

Dear Diary,

Let's set the record straight. I did not blab Ashley's secret. But does Ashley believe me? Noooo!

And boy – was she mad. After breakfast she dragged me all the way back to our room and let me have it.

"This is your way of getting even, isn't it?" Ashley demanded. "Because I'm winning your stupid bet and you're starting to wimp out!"

The words made my toes twist.

"Wimp out?" I asked. "What do you mean?"

"I'd tell you," Ashley said. She pointed to her watch. "But from this moment on we are not speaking."

"Give me a break!" I groaned. Ashley stomped out of the room.

I sat down on my bed and sighed. There was no way I could prove to Ashley that I didn't blab. But now that I felt braver, I could probably learn to scuba dive.

I changed into my red bathing suit. Then I marched out to the beach. Ashley and some of the campers were playing volleyball. Others were snorkelling in the ocean with Brad and Jenny.

"Mary-Kate!" Phoebe said. She was sitting on a beach blanket and shaking her head. "I'm trying to write about scuba diving, but all I can think of is sharks."

"Sharks!" I threw back my head and headed for the ocean. "I laugh in the face of sharks. Ha!"

"Mary-Kate?" Phoebe asked. "Where are you going?"

"For a swim!" I told her. "The sea is our friend, you know. Ask the Little Mermaid!"

Shore Thing

The waves crashed around my legs as I walked into the ocean. The water felt nice and cool against my sunburn. I walked deeper and deeper.

When I was in up to my waist I took a deep breath. I was about to dip myself when I saw something pink and shimmery on top of the water.

"Oooh," I thought. "That's beautiful." I stared at it as it floated closer and closer. . .

"Watch out!" a voice shouted.

I felt a hand grip my shoulder. I spun around and saw Devon. "Get away from that!" he ordered.

"Why?" I asked as we hurried to shore.

"That was a Man o' War!" Devon said. "The biggest, meanest jellyfish there is. You don't want to get stung by him!"

Man O'War!

My knees shook. My heart raced. I wanted to thank Devon, but my mouth was as dry as sawdust.

Who am I kidding, Diary?

In three days we take the scuba certification test – and I can't even put my head underwater!

Chapter 11

Tuesday

Dear Diary,

This morning Ross wasn't talking to me. And I wasn't talking to Mary-Kate. How could I after she blabbed my secret all over camp?

"Cheryl," I said at breakfast. "Please tell Mary-Kate to pass the guava jelly."

Mary-Kate turned to Cheryl. "Tell Ashley it isn't guava," she said. "It's pineapple!"

"Tell her yourself," Cheryl complained. "I'm out of here." She picked up her tray and left.

Ross didn't speak to me all through scuba class or marine biology. I was feeling worse and worse. Ross never did anything bad to me. And now I've embarrassed him in front of the whole camp!

At least I didn't mean to.

During our midday break Devon asked me to go to town with him. I just wanted to get away – so I said yes.

We got permission from Sid to borrow the camp bikes. Then we peddled up the road to town. Just the two of us.

"How about some ice cream?" Devon asked as we chained our bikes to a fence.

Shore Thing

"Cool!" I said. "I could go for mint chocolate chip in a waffle cone."

"Mint chocolate chip?" Devon cried. He wrinkled his nose and stuck out his tongue. "Yuck!"

I starred at him. Devon and I obviously had nothing in common.

Why would I like a boy who hates 4-You and mint-chocolate-chip ice cream?

Sure, Devon is cute. But there are lots of good-looking boys in the world. And only one Ross.

Ross loves 4-You and mint-chocolate-chip ice cream. And most important – he likes *me!*

"I *love* mint chocolate chip," I said firmly. "And I think I'll make mine a *double scoop!*"

Devon shrugged and ordered a vanilla cone for himself.

Vanilla? Boring!

Diary, now I have two goals: winning the bet and getting Ross back.

So wish me luck!

Dear Diary,
After seeing that Man o' War in the ocean yesterday I was happy to see the

swimming pool again. I even managed to get into the pool with my mask and tank on.

I quickly dunked my head underwater.

"Maybe there's hope," I told Phoebe after I climbed out of the pool. "Maybe I'm not such a chicken after all."

"Speak for yourself," Phoebe wailed. "I still haven't gone underwater yet."

"Okay, you guys!" Jenny called. "I have a surprise for you. Tomorrow afternoon you'll finally get to dive in the ocean!"

I remembered the Man o' War and began to sweat.

What if it were waiting for me? What if I stepped on one of its babies and now it wants revenge?

I gave my head a shake. I had watched way too many films on the Fright Channel!

"The ocean dive is all in preparation for your scuba test in two days," Jenny said.

"Scuba! Scuba! Scuba!" everyone cheered.

I glanced at Ashley cheering along.

"Look at her," I mumbled under my breath. "Miss Navy Seal."

Diary, this is more than I can take. Why am I suddenly the wuss and Ashley the superhero?

It's not just unfair – it's against the law of nature!

Chapter 12

Wednesday

Dear Diary,

When I woke up this morning the first thing I did was check my sunburn. It was a pale cotton-candy pink.

Not red enough to get me out of that ocean dive!

I could hear Ashley in the bathroom singing "Under the Sea" at the top of her lungs. To her, *The Worst That Can Happen* book is history. To me it's a constant reminder of things to come. *Disaster!*

Right after breakfast we suited up for the dive. Then we boarded Sid's special diving boat.

"Remember, divers!" Sid called as he sailed the boat out to sea. "If you find any sunken treasure I get a cut!"

"What if we find skeletons?" Jeremy called out.

Everyone laughed except Phoebe and me.

"Why don't they just make us walk the plank?" Phoebe groaned.

My stomach churned as the boat sailed farther and farther away from the shore. When it stopped after about a mile, Sid dropped an anchor. Then Jenny took over. She gave a talk about boat safety, then guided us to the diving platform.

"Now remember," Jenny said. "Breathe naturally

through your mouthpiece. That's the key."

My heart pounded as the campers jumped into the ocean one by one. Then it was my turn. I stood next to Jeremy on the platform and stared into the water.

"Go for it!" Jeremy said. He tapped my shoulder lightly. But I was so nervous I tumbled overboard!

I squeezed my eyes shut as I splashed into the water and began to sink. Water rushed all around me. I began to panic. But then I stopped falling and began to float.

Breathing through my mouthpiece I felt weightless. Almost as if I was on the moon!

My eyes popped open and I gasped. A school of neon fish swam past my mask. I looked around and saw electric-coloured fish everywhere. Tiny bubbles floated around mountains of coral and forests of underwater plants.

Holy mackerel, I thought. *This is awesome!*

Summer and Justin waved to me under the water. Then the three of us followed a school of catfish around a coral peak. Jenny was right – scuba diving was like visiting a whole new world. By the time I swam back to the

Shore Thing

surface I felt empowered and totally exhilarated!

Diary – spread the word.

Mary-Kate Burke went deep sea diving and loved it.

And she is back in the game!

Dear Diary,

Bad news.

Getting Ross back is not going to be as easy as I thought.

Today I tried everything. I wore the coral choker he gave me. I smiled at him so much my face hurt. I even sat next to him on Sid's diving boat.

"Do you believe we're going scuba diving under the ocean?" I asked Ross as the boat sailed out.

"Hmmph," Ross said.

Try again.

"I'm so psyched that you're coming to Chicago, Ross," I said. "I'll show you the Sears Tower and we can even see a Cubs game if you'd like—"

"Who says I'm still coming to Chicago?" Ross grumbled.

Uh-oh.

"But, Ross," I said. "What about the 4-You concert? We were going together, remember?"

"Why don't you just go with Mr. Florida Tan?" Ross snapped. "Devon Benjamin?"

The boat jerked and so did my stomach. I glanced at Devon on the other side of the boat. He was busy putting on sunscreen and talking to Justin.

I turned to Ross. I had to set the record straight once and for all.

"Devon doesn't even like 4-You," I said firmly. "Besides, you're the one I want to go with. Because you're the guy I like!"

Ross stared straight ahead as he leaned on a life belt. "You mean it?" he asked.

"Cross my heart and hope to die!" I said.

Ross broke into a smile.

"So will you come to Chicago this summer?" I asked.

"Maybe," Ross said.

"Maybe" wasn't as good as "yes." But it was better than "no"!

That was the last thing Ross said to me all day, but at least now I have hope. In fact, I even made up a list of reasons I want Ross back, so that I don't give up.

WHY I WANT ROSS BACK: He's nice. He makes me laugh. He's cute. He's a Gemini like me. He does

Shore Thing

an awesome impression of our headmistress, Mrs. Pritchard! He likes 4-You and mint-chocolate-chip ice cream.

Best of all, he really likes me. And I'd better work fast if I want to keep it that way!

Chapter 13

Thursday

Dear Diary,

Today there were no activities, so we could all spend the day studying for our scuba certificate test.

Before lunch, I saw Ashley cramming with Cheryl on a beach blanket. I wanted to join them but knew better. Ashley would just tell me to "be like an egg and beat it!"

I went to my room and tried to study buoyancy compensators and second-stage regulators. But something was missing. Not my notes. Not even the flannel shirt I always wear when I study for a test.

What was missing was Ashley!

You see, ever since Ashley and I were in third grade we've always studied together. And right before a test we would give each other our traditional good luck thumbs-up!

I lay back on my bed and gave a big sigh.

Why won't Ashley believe that I didn't blab her secret? And why can't this stupid fight be over once and for all?

Tossing my scuba textbook aside I picked up my diary. I opened it to the last page and froze. It wasn't my diary – it was Ashley's!

Shore Thing

"Whoops!" I tried to shut it. But my eyes became glued to a list called – WHY I WANT ROSS BACK.

"So Ashley still likes Ross!" I told myself as I read the list. "What do you know . . ."

I heard someone in the hall. Shutting the diary, I felt my heart pound. Ashley couldn't know I was reading her diary – even if it *was* by mistake!

"Fingerprints!" I hissed.

Grabbing a tissue, I rubbed the cover of the diary. But just as I was about to toss the tissue away I noticed a pile of pictures on the bottom of the wastebasket.

I shuffled through the pictures. They were Ashley's wildlife shots – the ones filled with Devon!

"So that's it," I said to myself. "Ashley is over Devon. Which is why she wants Ross back!"

Suddenly I had a brilliant idea. If I could help Ashley get Ross back, maybe she'd get over our fight!

I ran outside and looked for Ross. I found him swinging in a hammock behind the house.

"Hi, Ross!" I said.

Ross looked up from his scuba textbook.

"Hey, Mary-Kate," Ross said. He shifted over and made room for me to sit down. "What's up?"

I took a deep breath and got right to the point.

Two of a Kind Diaries

"Look, Ross," I said. "Ashley thinks you're great! She wants to be your girlfriend again."

Ross began to swing the hammock as he thought. "But what about Devon?" he asked. "What if Ashley still likes him?"

"Devon Shmevon!" I said. "If she likes him so much what are his pictures doing in the trash can?"

"Pictures?" Ross asked. "What pictures?"

"The pictures from the photography workshop," I explained. "I was sick that day, and you must have been at that shark film."

Ross's smile turned into a big frown. What did I say?

"Ashley told me she wasn't going to that workshop," Ross said. "She said she was going to spend the whole afternoon with you."

My jaw dropped open. How could I forget that Ashley didn't want Ross to know?

"Ashley *was* going to spend the afternoon with me," I said quickly. "But I was fast asleep. So who can blame her for splitting?"

Ross got up from the hammock so fast that it

Shore Thing

tipped back. I fell back on the ground with a THUNK.

"Where are you going?" I called out to Ross.

"To find Ashley," Ross called back. "And tell her my trip to Chicago is off. She *lied* to me!"

"Oh, noooo!" I groaned.

I lay on the ground and stared up at the puffy white clouds. All I wanted to do was make things better.

And now I had made things worse!

Dear Diary,

Motor-mouth Mary-Kate Burke did it again!

Telling everyone about my crush on Devon was bad enough. But telling Ross that I lied to him is downright criminal!

"You blabbed again!" I shouted to Mary-Kate in our room. "You told Ross that I went to that photography workshop!"

"I didn't mean to!" Mary-Kate pleaded. "I found out you wanted Ross back, and I wanted to help!"

"How did you find out?" I asked.

Mary-Kate gulped. "Your . . . d-d-diary."

"You read my diary?" I shrieked. "Our second rule as twins is not to read each other's diaries!"

"What's rule number one?" Mary-Kate asked.

"Not to use each other's toothbrushes," I said. "And don't you try to change the subject!"

"Okay, okay," Mary-Kate said. "I picked up your diary by mistake. And I only read one page!"

I folded my arms across my chest.

"You still can't deal with it, can you, Mary-Kate?" I asked. "You still can't accept that I'm winning our bet. So you'll do anything to make my life here the pits!"

"Oh, get real, will you?" Mary-Kate said. "This has nothing to do with our stupid bet!"

"And if you think the bet is off," I said coolly. "You are *wrong*!"

"Fine with me!" Mary-Kate said. "And may the best twin win!"

As I stormed out of our room I knew this wasn't just a bet any more. . .

This is *war*!

Chapter 14

Friday

Hi, Diary!

Here's a major news flash: I, Mary-Kate Burke, am now a certified scuba diver!

Early this morning we took the written test and in the afternoon we showed off our scuba skills in the pool.

The written test wasn't too tough (even though I had trouble spelling *buoyancy*). What was *really* tough was sitting just a few seats away from Ashley, knowing we weren't speaking to each other. We didn't even give each other our usual thumbs-up sign before the test!

No one knew the results of the test until after dinner. Jenny announced that everyone passed except for Phoebe. Everyone felt sorry for Phoebe, but we still hugged each other and gave high-fives.

Our gross cousin Jeremy dunked his face in his oatmeal and blew 'scuba' bubbles. Cute.

I saw Ashley at the other end of the table. I was still mad but didn't want this fight to go on forever. So I took a deep breath and walked over to her.

"Congratulations," I told her. "You did it."

Ashley frowned. Then she dropped a bombshell.

Two of a Kind Diaries

"Mary-Kate, when we get back to Chicago I'm going to ask Dad for separate rooms," she said. "You can stay in our room, and I'll move up to the attic."

What? Ashley was taking this too far!

"Don't you remember what happened once before when I moved up to the attic?" I asked her.

"I finally had a neat room for a change?" Ashley said.

"Ashley," I said. "When I moved up to the attic I thought I heard bats!"

"There are no bats in our house, Mary-Kate," Ashley said. "Only RATS!"

I felt my face turn red. Did she mean – me?

"Um, Ashley," Summer said. "You'd better finish your lemon sherbet. Before it gets cold."

I spun around and marched back to my side of the table. Not only is Ashley dragging this fight all the way to Chicago, she's still blaming me for something I never did!

And that stinks!

Shore Thing

Dear Diary,

Scuba! Scuba! Scuba!

Today I got my scuba certificate and it felt great. In fact, everybody passed the test except for Phoebe.

"You mean I failed?" Phoebe cried.

"Sorry, Phoebe," Jenny said. "But before you get your scuba certificate you have to go underwater."

Ross passed the test. So did Mary-Kate.

Which means Mary-Kate and I are both winning the bet. In fact, the score is practically tied.

But there's still hope.

This bet isn't just about passing the scuba test. It's also about doing well in every single camp activity.

There's still that canoe race on the swamp tomorrow. And if there are enough spiders and snakes, Mary-Kate might still freak!

Oh, well, Diary, gotta fly.

There's another beach party tonight. And if I'm lucky, Ross will accept my roasted marshmallow peace offering!

See ya!

Chapter 15

Saturday

Dear Diary,

The big canoe race came right after breakfast.

"You'll be split up into teams of two this time," Sid said when we reached the swamp. "All you have to do is follow the red flag markers until you reach the finish point. The first canoe that comes in – wins!"

I didn't ask Ross to team up. Last night at the party he refused to even talk to me. So I chose Elise.

Elise and I threw our backpacks into the canoe. Then we shoved our boat into the swamp and jumped in. Elise took the front. I took the back.

I looked over my shoulder at the others. Mary-Kate was getting into a boat with Phoebe.

The swamp became muckier and narrower as we paddled on. Soon there were no other canoes in sight. Just deer, pelicans, and squawking birds.

"Are you and Mary-Kate still not talking?" Elise asked as she worked her oar.

"Last I checked," I said.

"That's too bad." Elise sighed. "You don't know how lucky you are to have a twin sister."

"A twin that blabs!" I scoffed.

Shore Thing

"But Mary-Kate said she didn't tell!" Elise said.

"Then who did?" I asked.

"Beats me," Elise said. "When I went down to breakfast everybody was already talking about it. I think Jeremy started it."

"Then Mary-Kate told Jeremy," I said.

"Are you sure?" Elise asked.

"Mary-Kate and I were the only ones in the dining room when I told her about Devon," I said with a shrug.

Elise looked over her shoulder.

"Dining room?" she said. "That explains it!"

"Huh?" I asked.

"Taco the parrot!" Elise cried. "That blabbermouth with a beak repeats everything he hears!"

I stopped paddling and tried to remember everything Mary-Kate and I said to each other in the dining room.

Then it hit me.

"Elise!" I said. "Mary-Kate said 'Ashley loves Devon' a few times. And Taco was there!"

"Come to think of it," Elise said, "when we asked Jeremy how he knew, he said a little birdie told him. But who knew he meant a *real* bird?"

"Oh, great!" I groaned. But I wasn't mad at the

parrot. I was mad at myself for blaming Mary-Kate. And not listening to her when she told me she was innocent.

Maybe Mary-Kate was right about the diary, too, I thought. Maybe she *did* open it by accident. And maybe she *couldn't* help spilling the beans about the photography workshop.

"What are you going to do now?" Elise asked as we paddled under a canopy of moss.

"What else can I do?" I asked. "As soon as I see Mary-Kate I'm declaring a truce!"

"It's about time!" Elise said. "Now let's win this race!"

I smiled as I pushed my oar into the soupy swamp. I was wrong about Mary-Kate. But it wasn't too late to make things right!

Elise and I didn't win the race, but we came really close. Our canoe came in second and the counsellors greeted us at the finish point with cheers and a yummy barbecue.

And the reason I'm writing to you is that Mrs. Clare had to drive back to the house for some hot dog buns. I helped her grab a few bottles of ketchup, then ran up to my room to find you.

I expected to see Mary-Kate at the barbecue

Shore Thing

when we got back, but she and Phoebe were a no-show. In fact, practically all of the canoes were in except for theirs.

Oh, well, I thought. Maybe Mary-Kate did freak. She and Phoebe probably just slowed down.

I smiled to myself as I poured ketchup on my burger. The fight may be over.

But the bet was still on!

Dear Diary,

It's a good thing I found you in my backpack, Diary, because you will never believe where I am now.

Give up? I'm stuck in the middle of a swamp!

How did I go from being a camper to a castaway in just a matter of hours? Let me tell you...

After Phoebe and I jumped into our canoes we got a good start. And after already canoeing once, we sort of knew the drill.

"Just keep your eyes on those red flags," I told Phoebe. "And we'll be at the finish point in no time."

"You've become so brave lately, Mary-Kate," Phoebe sighed. "What's your secret?"

"I stopped sweating," I said with a smile. "And started *doing*."

Two of a Kind Diaries

The swamp got thicker and smellier as we kept paddling. I could hear bullfrogs, birds, and lots of crickets.

"I can't believe I failed that scuba test yesterday!" Phoebe said as she pushed the oar through the water.

"You can probably take a scuba course when you get back to San Francisco," I said.

"Who cares about scuba?" Phoebe cried. "It's my article I'm worried about."

"Your article?" I asked.

"I was going to write about my adventures in scuba diving," Phoebe said. "What do I write about now? Beach fashions? Conch chowder? The stuffed alligators in the gift shop?"

"You'll think of something, Phoebe," I said.

As the swamp became narrower the moss on the trees hung lower and lower. I saw a red flag to the right.

"Hang on," I told Phoebe. "This is where we saw those spiders the last time."

"Spiders!" Phoebe stopped paddling. "I can't go under those spiders again. I can't!"

I rested my oar and looked over my shoulder.

Shore Thing

Poor Phoebe was shaking in her 1960s Keds madras trainers.

"What do you want to do?" I asked Phoebe. "It's not as if we can turn around."

"Then let's take another route!" Phoebe pleaded. She looked around and pointed. "There!"

I looked to see where Phoebe was pointing. A narrow channel ran off in another direction. It was flanked by tall swamp grass.

"Come on, Phoebe," I said. "We wouldn't be following the flags if we went that way."

"Brad said the swamp was circular," Phoebe said. "So we'll end up in the same place sooner or later."

"No, Phoebe—"

It was too late. Phoebe was turning the canoe the other way.

"Okay, okay!" I said. "But let's just hope you're right about that circular swamp."

We paddled and paddled for what seemed like forever. The swamp water in the channel became thick as paste. And soon our canoe was stuck in a tangle of mangrove roots!

"I think we're stuck," Phoebe gulped.

"And *lost*!" I declared.

"Lost?" Phoebe gasped. "What do we do?"

"We wait for help, that's what we do!" I said.

Two of a Kind Diaries

A frog jumped into our canoe. It was too much to take, so we climbed out and walked along a giant root leading to a mossy island.

While Phoebe sat hugging her knees I took out my diary. I figured the only way to keep calm was to write.

"You know, Mary-Kate," Phoebe said softly. "Robinson Crusoe had a diary, too."

"Robinson Crusoe?" I wailed. Robinson Crusoe was stranded on an island for decades. By the time they found him, his clothes were tattered and his beard was a mile long. But at least he had coconuts!

"Mary-Kate!" Phoebe said, her dark eyes flashing behind her glasses. "If no one finds us soon we're toast!"

"We should be so lucky," I muttered. "If no one finds us – we're gator chow!"

We sat in silence looking out at the swamp. Diary, the worst that can happen – is now happening to us!

Dear Diary,
I have awful news!

Shore Thing

We waited and waited and waited for Mary-Kate's and Phoebe's canoe to come in, but it never did. Now Sid and the counsellors are setting up a search party.

A search party!

Oh, Diary!

Why did I say those horrible things about Mary-Kate? Why didn't I believe her when she said she didn't blab? And what if they never find her again?

What will I ever do without my sister?

Two for the Road

by Nancy Butcher

📖 HarperCollins*Entertainment*
An Imprint of HarperCollins*Publishers*
A PARACHUTE PRESS BOOK

Chapter 1

Saturday

Dear Diary,

Help! Mary-Kate is missing!

Oh, Diary, I never thought I'd be writing to you with such awful news. Mary-Kate and our friend Phoebe Cahill have been missing all day. They went canoeing in an alligator-filled swamp and never came back. The camp counsellors are organising a search party. I'm in my room, waiting for them to come and get me.

Mary-Kate, Phoebe, and I are in the Florida Keys, in a place called Camp Coral Reef. It's part of a special summer field trip that was arranged by our school, the White Oak Academy for Girls.

There are three other First Formers from White Oak: Summer Sorenson, Cheryl Miller and Elise Van Hook. Plus, there are five First Formers from the Harrington School for Boys: our cousin Jeremy Burke, Seth Samuels, Justin Martinez, Ross Lambert and Devon Benjamin, who's starting at Harrington in the fall. "First Form" is what they call seventh grade at White Oak and Harrington.

Two of a Kind Diaries

Camp Coral Reef isn't the sort of camp where you do crafts and play Capture the Flag and sleep on rock-hard bunks. Our "dorm" is this super-cool beach house with wicker furniture and a wrap-around porch that overlooks the ocean. For the last two weeks we've been studying wildlife photography, deep-sea fishing, and scuba-diving.

Anyway, it began right after we got here. Mary-Kate and I made this dumb bet. I happened to say a  few things about scuba, like how diving too deep can make your lungs explode and your eyeballs pop out. And how I wasn't crazy about the idea of being chased by thirty-foot alligators. It's not like I made this stuff up. I got it out of a really scientific book called *The Worst That Can Happen.*

Well, Mary-Kate took all this the wrong way.

"What a wuss!" she said with a laugh. "I bet you're not going to pass your scuba test. I bet you won't even make it through the next few weeks of camp. You'll be too scared to do anything!"

"A wuss?" I gasped. "I am not a wuss! I bet I can totally ace all this camp stuff! Not only that, I'll pass my scuba test . . . the first time!"

We hooked pinkies on that. Mary-Kate said

Two for the Road

whoever lost the bet would have to clean the winner's side of her dorm room for six whole months. That seemed a little harsh, especially since her side of the dorm room looks like her wardrobe exploded or something. I was pretty confident I was going to win, though, so I didn't put up too much of a fuss.

But things went downhill after that. *Way* downhill. I got really wrapped up in winning the bet. I also got a tiny bit wrapped up in the new guy, Devon Benjamin. Devon's from Daytona Beach, and he's super-nice, *plus* he's really, really cute. I should never have started thinking about him that way, though. I already *have* a boyfriend: Ross Lambert.

Well, I can't say it was all my fault.

The only person who knew about my Devon crush was Mary-Kate. And guess what? Mary-Kate blabbed my secret to the whole world, and Ross found out!

I got over my crush on Devon really fast. I discovered that we had nothing in common. He doesn't like mint chocolate-chip ice cream, and he doesn't like the band 4-You, either. Some people have no taste!

But Ross didn't get over being mad at me. Mary-Kate and I got into a big fight because of that. I accused her of blabbing my secret because she saw I was winning our bet. Mary-Kate insisted that she was innocent, but I didn't believe her.

Then two days ago she made things even worse between Ross and me. Mary-Kate said she was only trying to help. But I didn't believe that, either.

Mary-Kate and I stopped speaking to each other after that. Actually, that's not true. We stopped speaking to each other *after* I told her that when we got back home to Chicago, I was going to ask Dad for separate rooms because she was a total rat.

Now I know that nothing I accused Mary-Kate of is true. Oh, Diary, how could I have said those terrible things to her? How could I have let this stuff with Ross and Devon come between us? I mean, boys are important, but a sister is for ever.

And now she's missing! We had a big Camp Coral Reef canoe race this morning. Everyone finished by lunchtime – except for Mary-Kate and Phoebe, who didn't finish at all.

Where could they be? Will I ever see my sister again?

Got to go, Diary. Sid Pepper, the camp director, just knocked on my door and said that the search party's ready to roll.

This is *not* the kind of party I had in mind for our last weekend at Camp Coral Reef. Oh, Diary! We have to find them. We just *have* to.

Two for the Road

Dear Diary,

This is probably the last time I'll be writing to you.

Unless someone comes and rescues us, fast!

Diary, you'll never guess where I am. Phoebe and I are stuck on an island in the middle of a swamp. That's why there are little dead mosquitoes smushed all over the page.

Phoebe and I were teammates in the Camp Coral Reef canoe race. We were doing just great, following the little red flags that Sid and Brad and the other camp counsellors set up for the course.

But then we got to a place in the swamp where there were lots of spiders' webs stretched across the water – like the ones in those fake haunted houses, except these weren't fake. Phoebe said there was no way she was going under the spiders. I kind of agreed with her. So we took a different route.

Big mistake! We paddled and paddled for what seemed like forever. The swamp kept getting narrower and windier and slimier and soupier. We couldn't find any red flags, and we couldn't find any other canoers, either. It seemed as if we were the only ones for miles around.

Finally our canoe jammed into a bunch of mangrove roots. Mangroves are these gnarly trees that grow out of the water. No matter what we did, we couldn't get our canoe loose.

"I think we're stuck," Phoebe gulped.

"And lost!" I declared.

I stood up in the canoe and cupped my hands around my mouth. "Help!" I yelled.

Phoebe joined in. "Heeellllp!"

But there was no answer.

We finally gave up. We didn't know what else to do, so we abandoned ship and walked across a giant mangrove root over to this island. If you can call it that. It's just a big mound of moss and weeds with some bullfrogs, horseshoe crabs, and a whole lot of mosquitoes living on it.

We sat down on a spot that wasn't too slimy.

"If no one finds us soon, we're toast!" Phoebe announced grimly.

"If no one finds us, we're gator chow!" I corrected her. Florida, especially this part of Florida, is full of alligators – and other dangerous creatures, too.

So now we've been sitting here for a long time staring out at the swamp. Once in a while a pelican

Two for the Road

or a heron swoops down and checks us out. I've been having all sorts of dark, morbid thoughts. Like, even if we *don't* end up being gator chow (or crocodile chow or panther chow), how are we going to survive? I have half a protein bar in my backpack. Phoebe has three breath mints. We have a small bottle of cranberry juice. And I don't see anything to eat or drink on our little island, unless we're in the mood for bullfrog sushi or slimy green swamp water.

"Phoebe?" I said after a while. "Are we going to starve to death?"

"Don't even *say* that!" Phoebe cried out. "We can't give up!"

She jumped to her feet and headed back out to the canoe. She tried to pry it loose. "It's really, really stuck," she called out.

"I think we'd better start making a will," I said miserably. "You know, in case we don't . . . survive. I could write it down in my diary. Maybe someone will find it someday."

Phoebe sat down next to me again. "If something happens to us, I'm going to leave all my vintage black dresses to Ashley," she declared. Phoebe is a vintage *anything* nut and has an amazing collection of old clothes, jewellery, and shoes. Right now she was wearing khaki shorts, a green safari hat, and a

Two of a Kind Diaries

pair of Keds madras trainers from the 1960s.

At the mention of Ashley's name, I felt this awful pang. As of this morning, Ashley and I weren't speaking to each other. I was hoping we'd get a chance to make up after the canoe race.

But now I'm not sure we'll ever get the chance!

"I'm going to leave Ashley my Derek Jeter poster, my favourite glove, and all my CDs," I said in a choked-up voice.

"You'd better start writing this stuff down," Phoebe urged.

"O-okay." I turned to a fresh page and started writing:

LAST WILL AND TESTAMENT

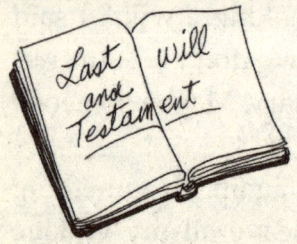

WE, MARY-KATE BURKE AND PHOEBE CAHILL, LEAVE THE FOLLOWING ITEMS TO OUR BELOVED FRIENDS AND FAMILY MEMBERS:
TO ASHLEY BURKE, PHOEBE LEAVES HER COLLECTION OF VINTAGE BLACK DRESSES, AND MARY-KATE LEAVES HER DEREK JETER POSTER, HER FAVOURITE GLOVE, AND HER ENTIRE CD COLLECTION.

Two for the Road

Phoebe read over my shoulder, then started giggling.

"What?" I demanded. "What is so funny about me leaving Ashley my stuff?"

"It's not that," Phoebe said. "I just thought of something we could leave Summer. A dictionary!"

I grinned. "Yeah! If she had a dictionary, she wouldn't get all those hard words mixed up."

"Like *initials* and *initiations*." Phoebe did a perfect imitation of Summer's voice. "'I have a fourteen-carat-gold necklace with my initiations on it! SVS, for Summer Victoria Sorenson!'" We both cracked up.

"We could leave Cheryl a copy of *Cooking-101 for Dummies*, since she's such a bad cook," I suggested. "Remember those brownies she made that time? They tasted like . . . like . . ."

"Baked swamp slime!" Phoebe laughed.

I nodded and wrote it all down, word for word. "Hey, I thought of something we could leave Seth! A subscription to *GuyStyle* magazine, since he wears such geeky clothes!"

"And don't forget Ross! We could leave him a dartboard with Devon Benjamin's picture on it!"

We went on like this for a long time. I was writing like mad, recording it all. I know we were saying some pretty mean things about our friends. But it made us laugh.

I heard a noise. It sounded like . . . thunder. I glanced up at the sky. It had got really dark. A storm was coming!

I stared at the dark sky, and at the murky green swamp, and at our canoe that was totally stuck in the mangroves. I realised that more than anything, at that moment, Phoebe and I needed to laugh.

I was just about to tell Phoebe what we should leave my cousin Jeremy when we heard *another* noise. A splashing noise.

I just heard the noise again. It sounds like something coming towards us in the water.

It sounds like an alligator!

Chapter 2

Sunday

Dear Diary,

I know you're dying to find out what happened yesterday. I would have told you last night, except I was totally wiped out after our big rescue mission. Being a hero is hard work!

So here's the scoop, Diary. (I'm writing this while I chow down on a bowl of papaya-kiwi oatmeal, so bear with me.)

Four of us went out in canoes to look for Mary-Kate and Phoebe. Sid and I were in one canoe. Jenny and Brad, two of the camp counsellors, were in the second canoe.

We paddled through the swamp for a really long time. There was no sign of my sister or Phoebe anywhere.

"Mary-Kate! Phoebe! Where are you?" I shouted their names over and over again until my voice was croaky.

But they didn't answer. The only sounds we heard were birds squawking and bullfrogs twanging.

The sky was getting darker, even though it was

the middle of the afternoon. "Looks like it might storm," Brad called out from the other canoe.

"Doesn't look good," Sid agreed.

After a while, we went around a bend in the channel and came to a sort of fork. We paddled to the left, following the little red flags. But then I noticed something.

"Sid? See those spiders' webs up there?" I said.

"Uh-huh. Just keep your head down, they won't bother you," Sid replied. "All the canoes went under them this afternoon."

"So did I," I said. "But Mary-Kate *hates* spiders, and so does Phoebe. There's no way *they* would have gone that way!"

Sid stopped paddling. "Wait up!" he called out to Jenny and Brad. "You mean, you think they would have taken the *right* fork? Even though the red flags point to the left?" he asked me.

"Uh-huh." I pointed my paddle at the narrow channel to the right. "I bet you anything they went that way – and got lost!"

So we all backed up and took the right fork. The channel was skinnier in that direction. There were mangrove roots all over the place, sticking out of the water like black claws.

All of a sudden I noticed a family of alligators

Two for the Road

hanging out on the banks of an island. "S-Sid?" I squeaked.

"Let's just keep paddling, okay?" he said in a tense voice.

"No problem!" I got down on my knees and started paddling extra-fast, as if I were in the Canoe Olympics or something. "Mary-Kate! Phoebe! Where are you guys!" I yelled hoarsely.

From far away I heard a voice reply.

"Sid, stop paddling!" I demanded.

Sid put his paddle down. So did Jenny and Brad. Everyone listened intently.

We all heard it then. *"Ashley! Hellllpp!"*

"That's my sister!" I cried out. "Mary-Kate! Phoebe! Hang on, we're coming for you!"

"We're over here! Hellllpp!"

The four of us paddled like crazy, following the sound of Mary-Kate's voice. We paddled and paddled until we reached this mossy little island.

All of a sudden there was a flash of lightning, then a crack of thunder. Just as the sky lit up, I saw Mary-Kate and Phoebe. They were on the banks of the island, jumping up and down and waving their arms.

Two of a Kind Diaries

I leaped out of the canoe and ran across the mangroves. "I thought you guys had got eaten by alligators!" I sobbed as I hugged Mary-Kate.

"I thought you guys *were* alligators when I heard your canoe."

Phoebe wrapped her arms around both of us. "I'm so glad you found us. I guess I won't have to leave you my vintage black dresses, after all!"

I stared at her. "Huh?"

"That's not important any more," Mary-Kate said. "I'm just so glad you found us!"

And I had my sister and my friend back, safe and sound!

Dear Diary,

Life sure seems different when you've had a near-death experience! Now that I've survived alligators, crocodiles, panthers, and near-starvation, I really appreciate the little things more. Like hot oatmeal for breakfast. Like having a real bed to sleep in. Like hanging out with my friends.

Like having the best twin sister in the whole world!

Two for the Road

Ashley and I are speaking to each other again – isn't that great, Diary? After the big rescue yesterday, we all canoed like mad back to Camp Coral Reef. Which was a good thing, since as soon as we hit shore, the skies opened up. We're talking thunder, lightning, the works.

It's so weird! I thought Phoebe and I were gone for twelve hours or something. But it turned out it was only five or six hours from the beginning of the canoe race to the time we got back.

Ashley and I rushed back to our room and took long, hot showers. Afterwards, we just hung out in our robes, gave each other pedicures (Tropical Tangerine!), and had a serious heart-to-heart talk.

"I'm sorry I accused you of messing things up with Ross and me," Ashley added. "I know you were only trying to get us back together."

And then it was *my* turn to apologise. I confessed that I *had* been jealous and cranky these last two weeks because Ashley was winning our bet. She was acing our scuba class, while I was making up all kinds of excuses so I could skip class and hole up in my room.

"After calling *you* a wuss, it turned out that *I* was the real wuss," I said sheepishly.

"It doesn't matter now, because in the end, we

both got our scuba certificates," Ashley pointed out.

So we hugged each other and swore that we would never, never, *never* let anything come between us again.

So that's the dramatic, nail-biting ending of our Camp Coral Reef vacation. And now we're about to start on Vacation Number Two – in Miami!

Tomorrow morning, bright and early, we're all saying goodbye to Camp Coral Reef and taking a bus to Miami. We're spending two weeks there before going home for the rest of the summer.

And guess what else? Mrs. Clare, our assistant headmistress from White Oak, said that we were going to be doing something really amazing in Miami. She wouldn't give us any details, though. She said she'd tell us tomorrow.

I'll keep you posted, Diary!

Chapter 3

Monday

Dear Diary,

You'll never believe where I am. Miami! In a huge hotel on the beach with two pools and room service and really cute lifeguards.

Mary-Kate and I have a balcony outside our room where we can watch the sun set over the ocean each night. Total bliss.

Camp Coral Reef already seems like it's a million miles away. We said goodbye to Sid and Brad and Jenny and all the counsellors this morning. Then we got on a bus and drove up the Intercoastal Highway to Miami.

On the bus Mrs. Clare made the big announcement about what we were going to be doing there.

"There will be a four-day sports tournament," she explained. "White Oak and Harrington will join together and form a team. You will compete against seven schools from all over the East Coast."

Mary-Kate and I stared at each other. A sports tournament! Luckily, I was in killer shape from my two weeks of canoeing, scuba-diving, and Frisbee-playing at Camp Coral Reef.

"I just found out about the tournament myself,"

Mrs. Clare went on. "I thought it sounded like fun."

Jeremy raised his hand. "What is it, like a triathlon or something?"

Summer frowned. "If it's a try-athlon, does that mean we only have to *try* doing it? Or what?"

"*Tri* means three, Summer. As in three sports," Mrs. Clare replied. "And yes, there actually *will* be three sports. Bicycling, beach volleyball, and water-skiing."

Phoebe raised her hand. "Can we pick which sport we want to participate in?" she asked, sounding a little nervous. "I mean, I've never even been water-skiing before."

I tried to imagine Phoebe bouncing over the waves in her vintage 1940s bathing suit, which sagged down to her knees. It wasn't easy.

"Different people will participate in different sports," Mrs. Clare said. "But in any case, don't worry if you're not experienced. The emphasis is on team spirit, cooperation, and having fun. The tournament is going to raise money to save Florida wildlife. For every team that finishes, the sponsors will donate

Two for the Road

a thousand dollars to the Wildlife Fund."

"Don't *we* get anything for all our hard work?" Jeremy grumbled.

Mrs. Clare grinned. "The team that finishes first will win a special prize," she said. "I'm not sure what it is yet. We'll find out in the next day or two."

Mrs. Clare said that we would get the rest of the scoop when we got to Miami. Everyone on the bus started buzzing excitedly about the tournament. I turned to Ross, who was sitting behind me. "Isn't this awesome?" I said.

I gave him my best Let's Make Up smile and waited for him to smile back. I was hoping that he'd forgiven me by now, especially after I nearly lost my life trying to save Mary-Kate and Phoebe in the swamp. Well, okay, so maybe that's kind of an exaggeration.

But I guess he was still mad, because he just gave me an icy stare.

"Can't talk," he mumbled. "Busy reading."

I peeked over the back of my seat. He was holding a copy of *Florida Dentistry Today* – upside down! He probably grabbed it out of the seat pocket, just to avoid talking to me. Who was he kidding?

Two of a Kind Diaries

Well, at least I still had two weeks to get him to forgive me.

Now, if I could only figure out *how*!

Dear Diary,

Okay. Stay calm. Don't panic. Maybe it's not as bad as it seems.

I'm writing this on hotel stationery. Because my real diary is . . . MISSING!!!

Let me take a deep breath and start at the beginning.

This morning we all piled on the bus for Miami. I tossed my suitcase in the storage space under the bus along with everyone else's and took a seat next to Ashley. Then I started to rummage through my backpack for my diary.

It wasn't there.

I was pretty annoyed. But I figured I probably left it in my suitcase. No big deal.

But the first thing I did when I got to our hotel room was unpack my suitcase and fish through it.

Still no diary.

It was all I could think about during lunch. Everyone else was by the pool chowing down on shrimp salad sandwiches and gabbing about the

Two for the Road

tournament. But I snuck away so I could come back to my room and go through everything again.

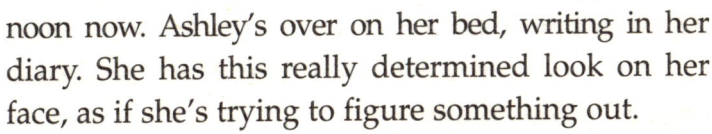

Still no diary.

It's the middle of the afternoon now. Ashley's over on her bed, writing in her diary. She has this really determined look on her face, as if she's trying to figure something out.

"Maybe he's at the pool right now," Ashley murmured.

"Huh?"

"Ross. Maybe he's at the pool. Hey, you want to go for a swim?" Ashley looked at me hopefully.

"If you're planning to win Ross back, you probably don't want my help," I told her. "I've been pretty useless so far."

Ashley said something about wearing her new red tankini, but I was only half-listening. All I could think about was my diary.

My eyes zoomed over to Ashley's backpack, which was lying next to her. Maybe I put my diary in her backpack by mistake. Should I tell Ashley it's missing? Or should I just search her backpack when she isn't looking?

Maybe I shouldn't worry so much. I don't want

Two of a Kind Diaries

Ashley to know I'm totally freaked out. And hey, what could I have written that's so bad?

Ha! A lot.

Let's see. I wrote that Summer needed a dictionary because she's always mixing up words. I also wrote that Cheryl was a terrible cook, and that Elise was as flaky as apple pie. And wasn't there something about how Justin could use a lifetime supply of breath mints?

It's not like I *meant* to write down those mean things. But Phoebe and I thought we were never going to make it back alive!

And I thought being lost in an alligator-filled swamp was bad.

No one can ever find out what I wrote in my diary. If they do, I might as well give up and go back to Chicago – for good. My life at White Oak would be over.

No one would ever talk to me again!

Chapter 4

Tuesday

Dear Diary,

This morning we all went on a boat ride in Biscayne Bay – except for Jeremy, who had a stomach ache from eating too much Key lime pie last night and had to stay in his hotel room. Jeremy really, *really* likes to eat.

Captain Sal, the captain of the S.S. *Clambake*, gave us a guided tour. He took us past islands with big, fancy mansions on them. And he told us the names of all the exotic-looking birds that we saw: ibiss, snowy egrets, and roseate spoonbills. Wow! Back in Chicago all we ever see are pigeons.

It was a picture-perfect day. The sun was shining. The sky was blue. Palm trees were swaying in the breeze. And I was wearing my cute new sundress with tropical fish all over it.

Ross was standing at the railing, staring out at the water. He looked as if he was deep in thought about something. It was my big chance.

I sauntered over to him. "Hey," I said cheerfully. "Isn't this fun?"

Ross shrugged. "I guess. Sure." He didn't even

bother to turn his head and look at me.

"How's your hotel room?"

"Fine."

"Who did you end up getting for a roommate?"

He mumbled something.

I frowned. "What?"

"Devon Benjamin," he said through clenched teeth.

"Oh."

I could feel my cheeks turning all red. Across the deck Devon was talking to Elise and Cheryl and pointing to some dolphins that were swimming near the boat. They were hanging on to his every word. Elise and Cheryl, that is – not the dolphins.

"Listen, Ross," I pleaded. "Can't we talk about this?"

"Talk about *what*?"

My heart sank. He wasn't going to make this easy for me. I looked around for Mary-Kate, hoping for an encouraging thumbs-up. But she was off in the corner with Phoebe, whispering like mad about something. What was up with that?

"Ross," I said softly. "I don't like Devon. I like *you*. Devon and I were just— "

"Look! That manatee's in trouble!" Devon interrupted my speech.

Two for the Road

"Where?" Mrs. Clare cried out. She was holding on to her enormous hat with the plastic fruit on it so it wouldn't blow away in the breeze.

Everyone rushed over to where Devon, Elise, and Cheryl were standing. "See that fishing boat over there?" Devon said, pointing. "There's a manatee caught in its net!"

"That's awful!" Mary-Kate ran over to us.

We learned all about manatees at Camp Coral Reef. They're these big marine mammals. And when I say big, I mean big – like ten feet long and a thousand pounds.

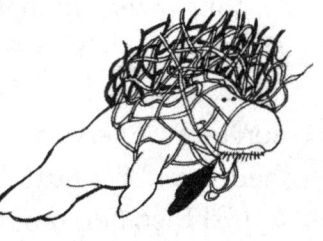

Sid told us that manatees are really cool, gentle animals. They're even vegetarians! The problem is, they're endangered, and they're becoming more endangered all the time.

"Can we help get it loose?" I asked Devon anxiously.

Just as I said that, the manatee wriggled out of the net and swam away all on its own. It was so cute, like an elephant with flippers!

It blinked at us, then disappeared under the water.

"Oh, good, he's all right," Summer said with a

Two of a Kind Diaries

sigh of relief. "It *is* a he, right? What do they call the female ones? Womanatees?"

"They're *all* called manatees," Devon said. "And it may *not* be all right. If it got cut by the net, which can sometimes happen, the cut can get infected. And then the manatee can die from the infection."

"What!" Cheryl exclaimed.

Devon looked pretty upset. "That's part of the reason why manatees are becoming extinct. Fishermen aren't always careful about where they throw their nets and lines into the water. Manatees don't move very fast, and they can get tangled up in them – and get hurt."

Just then I kind of forgot about my problems with Ross. I forgot about everything except for the poor manatee. I really hoped that it was going to be okay.

"Mrs. Clare?" Elise said quietly. "The tournament is going to make lots of money for the Wildlife Fund, right?" I knew just where she was going with that. Elise was a lot like her parents, who were Peace Corps volunteers in Fiji. She was always eager to help others, including animals.

"Right," Mrs. Clare said, nodding. "You're all going to be doing a little something to help save the manatees and other Florida wildlife, too. If you finish, that is."

Two for the Road

We are going to finish! I thought. And maybe we'll take first place! After seeing the manatee, I was super-determined to make that happen.

After a while Captain Sal turned the S.S. *Clambake* around and headed back to the marina. As he docked the boat, Mrs. Clare gave us more details about the tournament. We were really pumped up about it.

"There will be a big meeting about the tournament tomorrow morning, with all the other schools in attendance," she explained as we gathered on the dock. "Then, on Thursday morning, we'll have our *own* meeting. At that meeting our team captain will pick who's going to participate in the three different sports." She smiled. "But first you're all going to have to pick a team captain."

Team captain? I thought. That would be me!

Okay, so I'm not all that great at volleyball. But I'm a whiz on a bicycle. And I learned to water-ski on Lake Michigan near Chicago.

But none of that really matters, anyway. What I do best is motivate. Organise. Inspire.

I nudged Mary-Kate. "Nominate me," I whispered.

Mary-Kate seemed startled. She must have been thinking of something else. But just as she began to raise her hand, we heard a familiar voice behind us. Much too familiar.

"Hi, guys," Dana Woletsky called out. "What's up?"

Oh, no! What was *she* doing here?

Heads whipped around. A big white yacht was docking alongside the S.S. *Clambake*. Dana was standing on deck, wearing a killer blue sundress and supercool-looking shades. Her mom was at the helm, and her dad was tugging on the sails. I recognised them from the times they visited Dana at White Oak.

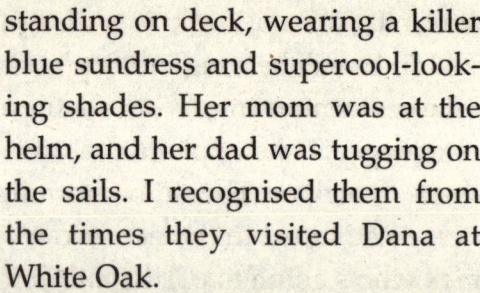

Dana was a White Oak First Former, too. She and I weren't exactly best buds. It all started when Mary-Kate and I transferred to White Oak from our school in Chicago. I asked Ross to the Sadie Hawkins Dance. Dana accused me of stealing Ross away from her. She had this idea that he was *her* boyfriend. Which was totally not true. But ever since then she's had it in for me.

Dana came down and joined us on the dock. Her mom and dad followed with a couple of Dana's suitcases. Summer ran up and gave Dana a big hug. Ross waved at her.

Two for the Road

Mrs. Clare beamed. "Dana! We're so glad you made it!"

"I didn't know you were going to be on this trip," I blurted out to Dana.

Dana glared at me.

Mrs. Clare smiled and said, "Dana's family arranged to return early from a cruise in the Bahamas so Dana could join us for the Miami leg of the trip," she explained. "And just in time to help us choose a team captain!"

Summer's hand shot up. "I nominate Dana," she said.

"I second her," Ross said.

"What?" I gasped.

"I nominate Ashley," Mary-Kate said quickly.

"I second her," Phoebe said.

I held my breath and waited for Ross to say, "I change my mind, I want *Ashley* to be team captain!" Or something like that. But he didn't say a word.

Oh, Diary! How could Ross side with Dana after all we've been through together? I know he's still angry with me about Devon. But he knows it was just a misunderstanding. Why can't he just get over it?

Anyway, Diary, we're going to vote on team captain tomorrow morning. I've got to get out there and drum up some support. So that means now I

Two of a Kind Diaries

have two goals. Beat Dana for team captain. And get Ross back!

Dear Diary,

It's official. I'm definitely doomed.

I've looked everywhere for the diary. I looked through Ashley's backpack, her suitcase, and her dressing table drawers, too. I looked through all my stuff for the sixth time.

There's no sign of it anywhere.

I'm writing this on a pad of hotel stationery. The guy at the front desk must think I have a lot of friends back home, because I keep asking him for more and more stationery.

I'm sitting in the Café Tango, which is a restaurant in the Little Havana section of Miami. Mrs. Clare brought us here for lunch after our boat ride on the S.S. *Clambake*.

Ashley's in a really crabby mood, even though I nominated her for team captain. I think it has something to do with the fact that Dana showed up out of the blue. Plus, Dana is sitting at a table with Summer and Elise – and Ross! Dana's parents were planning on heading off to Key West in their yacht, after they dropped her luggage off at our hotel. Too

Two for the Road

bad they didn't take Dana with them!

But I can't think about Ashley's problems right now. My problems are *way* bigger. I've hardly touched my black beans and rice and fried plantains because I'm so upset.

I kind of told Phoebe what was going on, during the boat ride, but she didn't seem to care too much.

"If Cheryl or Seth or someone finds your diary and reads our Last Will and Testament, we can just explain that we were temporarily insane," Phoebe said reasonably. "Who could blame us? We were staring death right in the face!"

Let's just say we agreed to disagree on this. After all, it's *my* diary. It's *my* handwriting. If anyone's going to take the fall for this, it's me!

I know, I know! There's a chance I dropped the diary on the beach by accident, and it's sinking to the bottom of the Atlantic Ocean as we speak. If I'm lucky.

But if I'm *not* so lucky, and one of my friends *does* have it, I have to get it back – pronto!

Chapter 5

Wednesday

Dear Diary,

This morning we had the big meeting for the sports tournament. Angela Velasquez, the sports director of the hotel, told us the deal while about a hundred of us munched down on bagels and cream cheese and guava smoothies on the beach.

"There are eight schools here from the East Coast that will be competing," she said. "Each school is responsible for choosing its own team captain by noon today."

Dana and I exchanged a glance. She flipped her hair over her shoulders and gave me a smug look, like she knew exactly who *our* team captain was going to be. We'd see about that!

Yesterday afternoon I bought a dozen big cookies at the bakery across the street from the hotel. I  bought a tube of blue icing, too, and wrote "Ashley for team captain!" on the cookies. I gave one to everyone in our group after dinner, along with a flyer that listed all the reasons why I would make a good team captain.

Two for the Road

Like:
- PROVEN LEADERSHIP QUALITIES!
- MOTIVATED TO WIN!
- DEDICATED TO THE CAUSE OF WILDLIFE!
- WILL WORK OVERTIME FOR YOU!

Everyone seemed pretty impressed by the cookies and flyers. Except for Summer, who is way too loyal to Dana. And Ross, who threw his cookie and flyer in the trash. Hmmm.

Angela held her clipboard in the air. "As you all know, the tournament will consist of three sports. Volleyball, water-skiing, and bicycling. We start on Sunday with round-robin volleyball. Monday will be the elimination volleyball event. Tuesday will be water-skiing. And we'll finish up on Wednesday with a 10K bike race."

Some guy in the back row stood up and raised his hand. I practically choked on my bagel. He was really super-cut, and he wore a T-shirt that said NO PAIN, NO GAIN. He looked as if he could bench-press two hundred pounds in his sleep.

In fact, a lot of the guys and girls in the crowd looked like pretty serious athletes. We – White Oak and Harrington – were in for some major competition!

"Does everyone compete in all three sports?" Mr. No Pain, No Gain asked Angela.

"No," Angela replied. She glanced quickly at her clipboard. "There are ten to twelve of you per school. Each school should have a maximum of six people competing in each sport. So it's up to the team captains to decide which six people will compete in each of the three sports."

Phoebe leaned over to me and whispered, "Do I really *have* to participate? Can't I just write about this for the *Acorn*?" She was the editor of the White Oak First Form newspaper and was always looking for stuff to write about.

"Mrs. Clare says we *all* have to participate in at least one of the events. *And* finish. Or the money doesn't go to the Wildlife Fund," I whispered back. "Don't worry, Phoebe. We'll get you a pair of spandex bike shorts with racing stripes. Vintage 1980s. It'll help you get into the spirit of things!"

"The team captains will have the next few days to decide who competes in which sport and to lead the practises for those sports." Angela grinned. "I'm sure your school chaperons have told you that the tournament's sponsors will donate one thousand

Two for the Road

dollars to the Wildlife Fund for every team that finishes. That means that if every team finishes, eight thousand dollars will go towards helping to save Florida wildlife!"

Everyone cheered. I raised my fist in the air and cheered, too.

"And there's more," Angela added. "Whichever school finishes first will get a special grand prize."

I held my breath. I wondered what it would be.

"The first-place school," Angela went on, "will win a trip to Seaquarium, where you'll get to name their brand-new baby manatee – plus swim with the dolphins!"

A baby manatee! Swimming with the dolphins! I couldn't believe it. Now I really, really, *really* wanted our team to win.

And I was just the person to lead us to victory!

After the big meeting was over, Mrs. Clare called our group aside. "Okay, gang. We have two nominations for team captain on the table. Let's take a vote."

Gulp! I glanced around. I knew Phoebe and Mary-Kate would vote for me. I knew Summer and Ross would vote for Dana, unless Ross had come to his senses and forgiven me.

I had no idea how Jeremy, Justin, Seth, Devon,

Two of a Kind Diaries

Elise, and Cheryl would vote, though. And what if it was a tie? *Then* what?

The big moment came. "All those for Dana Woletsky?" Mrs. Clare said.

A bunch of hands shot up. Summer, Ross, Elise, Seth, and Dana.

"You can't vote for yourself, Dana," Mrs. Clare told her. "Okay, that's four votes for Dana. All those for Ashley Burke?"

Phoebe, Mary-Kate, Jeremy, Justin, Devon, and Cheryl raised their hands.

Mrs. Clare smiled. "We have a winner! Ashley Burke will be our team captain!"

YESSSSSS!!!! It was all I could do to keep from jumping up and down and screaming for joy.

Mary-Kate high-fived me. "Way to go, sis!"

"Congratulations, Ashley!" Phoebe said, hugging me. "I can't wait to profile you for the *Acorn*."

Jeremy slapped me on the back. Hard. "I only voted for you because of the cookie."

"Thanks, Jeremy, I appreciate that," I said sweetly.

At that moment I would have been in a really good mood except for two things. (Well, three

Two for the Road

things, if you include Jeremy's comment.)

First, Ross didn't say a word to me. No "Congratulations." No "Good luck." No nothing.

And second, Dana *did* say a word to me. A bunch of words, in fact. And they sent a chill up my spine.

"If you think this team's going to finish, you are so wrong," she said. "Just you wait!"

What did she mean by that?

Dear Diary,

After lunch, while we were all hanging out at the pool, I told Ashley about the missing diary.

"What if someone has it?" I said miserably. "There are a *lot* of things in there that I wouldn't want anyone to read!"

But Ashley didn't seem too concerned.

"You probably dropped it somewhere back at Camp Coral Reefs," Ashley shrugged. "Some alligators probably chowed down on it. I wouldn't worry about it if I were you. I wonder if *this* would be a good practice schedule. . ." She nibbled on her pencil, then hunched over her clipboard and began scribbling like mad.

Okay, well, so much for sympathy. Phoebe wasn't worried, either. She was sitting in a lounge chair, wearing these huge bug-like sunglasses and reading a novel about Florida in the 1930s. Even when I reminded her about all the horrible things I wrote, she just told me again not to freak out about it.

Just then, I heard a noise in the bushes behind us. "What was that?" I said, turning around.

"Hmm?" Phoebe wasn't even paying attention. "What was *what*?"

I looked and looked, but I didn't see anything – or anyone – in the bushes. I guess I was just imagining things.

I peeked over the top of my shades and did a quick sweep of the pool area. Ross, Seth, and Justin were having a cannonball competition in the deep end. Devon was demonstrating jackknife dives for Elise and Cheryl off the diving board. Dana and Summer were sipping iced tea and flipping through a stack of fashion magazines.

So far no one had come up to me and said anything about my diary. Maybe Ashley and Phoebe were right. Maybe I did drop it in the swamp. Because if someone had it, we would have heard about it by now.

Two for the Road

But maybe they were wrong. Maybe the person who had it was just lying low. Biding time, trying to figure out the best time to attack.

This was driving me crazy. I couldn't just wait around for someone to get even with me. But what could I do?

Chapter 6

Thursday

Dear Diary,

Okay, so I came up with this brilliant plan to figure out who has my diary. *If* anyone has it, that is.

I figured that whoever has it would have read everything in it.

So I decided to go down the list of suspects, one by one, and ask each person a bunch of really sneaky, subtle questions. That way I could figure out if the person had read my diary or not.

I started with Cheryl. At breakfast I found her sitting alone on the terrace. She was writing postcards and picking at a bowl of oatmeal.

"Hey, Cheryl!" I pulled up a chair and sat down next to her.

"Hey, Mary-Kate."

"Writing some postcards?"

"Yeah, to my parents and my grandparents and my aunt Sally in Connecticut."

I nodded and smiled. I tried to remember what I had written in the Last Will and Testament about Cheryl. And then it came to me. *To Cheryl Miller, a copy of* Cooking 101 for Dummies, *because her*

Two for the Road

brownies taste like baked swamp slime...

I wondered how I was going to steer the conversation around to the subject of cooking. And then I noticed that Cheryl had cutely arranged the blueberries on the oatmeal so that they formed a smiley face. I saw my opportunity.

"That is so *cute*!" I gushed. "You have such a way with food!"

Cheryl gave me a funny look. "Uh, I just moved a few blueberries around. It's no big deal."

I laughed nervously. "Oh, but it's not just the blueberries! You are such an awesome cook!"

"I am?" Cheryl looked surprised.

I nodded. "You are! I remember those . . . those . . . *brownies* you made that time, for Elise's birthday. They were amazing!"

"They were?" Cheryl beamed.

"Did you get the recipe from a cookbook? You must use cookbooks, right?" I was really homing in on the dirt now.

Cheryl smiled and shrugged. "Not really. I kind of just eyeball everything. You know, a cup of this, a teaspoon of that, pop it in the oven, see what happens."

"How about that new cookbook? I thought you

might have it. *Cooking 101 for Dummies?"*

Cheryl's smile disappeared. *"Cooking 101 for DUMMIES?* Are you saying I'm a *dummy?"*

Oh, no! I realised that my sneaky, subtle interrogation had just taken a nosedive. "No, no, that's not what I meant! What I meant was—"

But it was too late. Cheryl picked up her bowl of oatmeal and her postcards and rose to her feet. "I think I'll eat *inside,"* she snapped.

Oops!

I guess I'm not as sneaky and subtle as I thought.

The good news is, it doesn't seem like Cheryl has my diary. One down, eight to go!

Dear Diary,

We had our team tryouts this morning after breakfast. I'd spent all yesterday afternoon and evening preparing for it, so I was ready. Raring to go, in fact.

"Okay, listen up!" I said loudly.

Everyone was gathered around the volleyball net. I was dressed in my new white SAVE THE MANATEES tank top, matching shorts, and visor, and I had a whistle around my neck. I looked *so* official.

"This morning I'm going to hold tryouts for the

three different sports," I explained. "Then tomorrow morning I'll announce who's going to be on which team."

Dana raised her hand. "You're going to pick me for the water-skiing team, right?" she said sweetly.

"You've got to try out, just like everyone else," I told her. Dana glared at me. "Any other questions before we get started?"

Summer fluttered her nails in the air. "I just had a manicure, so I really can't play volleyball. Could you pick me for one of the other sports?"

I sighed. Being a team captain wasn't easy. "Sorry, Summer, everyone has to try out for all three sports."

Jeremy raised his hand. "Hey, boss? How many hours a day are you going to make us practise?"

"Just in the mornings. In the afternoons we're all free to do whatever we want. We'll have practices tomorrow and Saturday. The tournament begins on Sunday."

After a few more questions we finally got started. I had everyone try out for volleyball, then water-skiing, then bicycling. Angela Velasquez had organised things so each school had the time, space,

Two of a Kind Diaries

and equipment necessary to hold the tryouts.

By the end of the morning I was covered with sand and sweat – and my clipboard was covered with notes. I had all three teams picked out – almost.

There was just one problem. Her name was Dana!

You'll never believe what she did during the tryouts, Diary. She wanted to be on the water-skiing team so badly that she actually *faked* being bad at volleyball and bicycling. I could tell she was faking – it was totally obvious. Plus, I knew from White Oak that she was good at those two sports.

The thing was, she wasn't good at water-skiing. She wasn't faking *that*. I was way better than she was. And I really wanted Devon and Cheryl on the water-skiing team, and Mary-Kate, Summer, and Jeremy, too.

That meant that I had to decide between Dana and me for the last spot on the water-skiing team. No one else even knew how to water-ski.

What was I going to do?

Chapter 7

Friday

Dear Diary,
   Yesterday afternoon, after the tryouts, a bunch of us decided to go Rollerblading in South Miami Beach. Or SoBe, as it's known to the locals.

   It was totally cool! There was a long boardwalk for Rollerblading that ran along the beach and Ocean Drive. It was lined with palm trees and tropical-looking flowers. Most of the women Rollerbladers we saw were wearing itty-bitty bikinis, and most of the guys were wearing Speedos. Holy cow!

   Phoebe was checking out something else altogether. "Look at the amazing Art Deco architecture!" she cried out.

   She pointed to the hotels and restaurants on Ocean Drive. I had never seen buildings that looked like that. There were pink buildings and baby-blue buildings and yellow buildings. A lot of them had chrome trim, old-fashioned neon signs, and pictures of flamingos on them.

   "I feel like we're back in the 1930s!" Phoebe sighed happily.

Two of a Kind Diaries

I wonder if the people in the 1930s wore bikinis and Speedos? I didn't think so!

I noticed that Ross was Rollerblading at the back, by himself. Ashley had stayed at the hotel, to do some serious brainstorming about who to pick for her three teams. I decided to take the opportunity to interrogate him. Maybe *he* had my diary?

I tried to remember what I had written in the Last Will and Testament about him. Oh, yeah.

To Ross Lambert, a dartboard with a picture of Devon Benjamin on it . . .

I dug in my stopper and waited until Ross had caught up. "Hey, Ross," I said with a smile.

"Oh, hi, Mary-Kate," he said. He didn't look totally thrilled to see me. "What's up?"

"Isn't this a blast?" I said cheerfully.

"Uh-huh."

"We should really get them to put in a Rollerblading path between White Oak and Harrington. Don't you think so?"

"Sure. I guess." He adjusted his helmet and gazed off in the distance, at a motorboat gunning through the water.

Okay, just go for it, I told myself. "So! What else do you like to do in your spare time, besides Rollerblade? Do you have any hobbies?"

Two for the Road

"Huh?" Ross stared at me. "Do I have any *hobbies*?"

"You know, like, stamp collecting, or piano playing, or bird-watching. Or what about darts? Do you like to play darts? Do you have a dartboard at home?"

"Uh, yeah, I have a dartboard." Ross was looking at me as if I were crazy. "I got one for Christmas last year."

"Really? Do you ever . . . ha ha . . . put a picture of anyone up on it? You know, like if you're mad at them or something?"

"A picture of . . . " Ross's eyes suddenly flashed. "Sure! Your sister gave me her school picture last fall. I think I know just what to do with it now! Thanks for the idea!" And with that he sped up until he was Rollerblading alongside Summer and Dana.

Great. Just what the Burke sisters needed – more bad PR with Ross Lambert!

But I wasn't going to be a quitter. I tried my sneaky, subtle approach two more times – with Seth and Elise.

I ended up putting my foot in my mouth with them, too! By the end of the day, I decided.

Two of a Kind Diaries

No more interrogations!

Dear Diary,

This morning I gathered the troops together on the beach and announced who was going to be on which team.

"The volleyball team will be Dana, Justin, Summer, Ross, Jeremy, and Mary-Kate," I said, reading off my clipboard.

Summer glanced at her nails. "I hope they're dry by now!"

"The bicycling team will be Phoebe, Ross, Dana, Elise, Seth, and me," I went on. I *had* to pick Phoebe, since that was the only sport she was willing to do. Ross was the best cyclist. Elise was the worst. But Elise had to be on the team, because she couldn't do the other two sports at all.

"Excellent!" Seth said. He and Ross exchanged high fives.

I took a deep breath. I noticed that Dana's eyes were boring holes into me.

"The water-skiing team will be . . ." I took another deep breath. "Devon, Cheryl, Mary-Kate, Summer, Jeremy. And me."

"*What!*"

That came from Dana. "Why aren't I on the

Two for the Road

water-skiing team?" she shrieked.

"I'm sorry, Dana. We can talk about this later."

Dana put her hands on her hips. "We can talk about it *now*! I demand an explanation!"

"Dana, not now." I tried to sound in charge. "Okay, everybody! The tournament starts in two days. We've got a lot to do. Here's how the practices are going to go. . . ."

Dana looked at me with pure fury. Then she leaned over and whispered something to Summer. Summer started giggling.

I raised my voice and tried to sound even more assertive. "I'm going to divide you all into your teams . . ."

I sent the bicycling team off, minus me, to do laps around the neighbourhood. I put Mary-Kate in charge of the volleyball team, to work on serves. I asked Devon to oversee the water-skiing team, to practise jumps. I had scheduled everything down to the last minute, so that the people who were on more than one team could split their time between sports.

We all worked hard for the next few hours. The sun was beating down, and the sand felt as though it had been baked. Clutching my clipboard, I went from team to team. I supervised, observed, took notes, and made suggestions for improvements.

Two of a Kind Diaries

When I got to the volleyball team, Mary-Kate called me aside. Everyone was taking a five-minute break to pour the contents of their water bottles over their heads.

"Dana's messing things up," she whispered. "Every time she gets the ball, she knocks it out of bounds. It's taking forever just to let everyone serve!"

I stared at Dana. She took a long swig from her water bottle, then stared at me.

"Is there a problem here, Dana?" I asked her.

Dana flipped her hair over her shoulders. "Problem? There's no problem!"

Ross walked up to Dana and tapped her on the shoulder. "You're not getting a good angle on the ball. Here, let me show you what I do. . ."

Dana slipped her hand through his arm. "Oh, that is so sweet, Ross, would you?" She gave me a mean smile.

Oh, Diary! Why did Dana have to show up in Miami????

Dear Diary,
   Things are bad. Really, really, *really* bad.

Two for the Road

Maybe I should pack my bags right now and fly back to Chicago and go into hiding – forever!

It turns out that someone has my diary, after all.

This afternoon, after practice, I went up to my hotel room to take a shower. There was an envelope under the door, addressed to me.

There was a note in it. The letters in the message had been cut out of a magazine and glued onto the paper. It said:

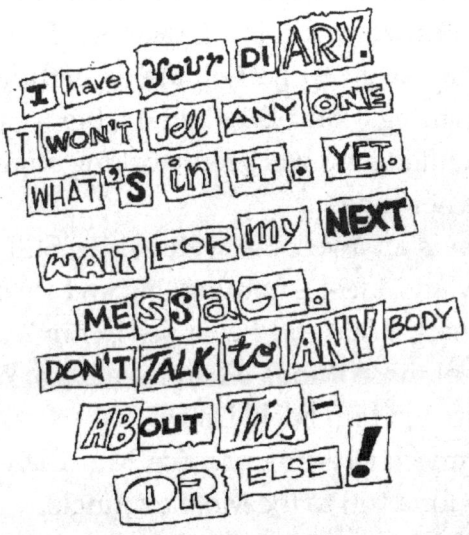

Chapter 8

Saturday

Dear Diary,

We had practice again this morning, and it went pretty well. Except that Dana didn't show up. She said she had a headache and had to stay in her room. And Mary-Kate was acting kind of distracted during her water-skiing runs. I wonder what's up with her? Tomorrow is the first day of the tournament! I really feel like our team is coming together. Even Phoebe, who didn't want to participate, is getting into the swing of things. And Elise, who's the weak link on the bicycling team, has been working super-hard to improve her times.

Devon is an awesome water-skier. Still, I look at him now and I feel – nothing. No sweaty palms, no racing heart. What did I ever see in him?

I *do* feel those things when I see Ross. Will I ever be able to win him back, Diary?

I had my chance after practice. Mrs. Clare rounded us all up for a trip to the Monkey Jungle.

The Monkey Jungle is kind of a zoo just for monkeys, gorillas, orangutans, gibbons, and other primates. The *really* cool thing is, the humans have to

Two for the Road

be in cages while the animals run around free!

I went up to Ross, who was checking out a bunch of macaques chasing one another up a palm tree. "Hey, Ross."

"Hey, Ashley," he said. Well, he was talking to me, anyway. There was hope!

"Those monkeys are pretty funny," I remarked.

"Yeah." There was a silence, then he added, "I really hope we win first place."

I smiled. "Yeah, me, too."

He started to say something else. But just then Dana came sauntering up to us. I guess she was feeling all better from her headache.

"Hey, Ross!" she said, giving him a big smile. She looped her arm through his. "Come here, I want to show you something!"

"Um, just a moment, I was in the middle of—"

"Come on, it'll just take a sec!" Dana brushed up really close to him and gave him another big smile.

Ross gave me an apologetic look, then the two of them went off. Ross said something to her, and she threw her head back and laughed.

Grrr!

Does Dana like Ross? Or is she just trying to

Two of a Kind Diaries

make me really, really upset? Because I have to tell you, Diary, it's working!

Dear Diary,

I hardly slept a wink last night because I was tossing and turning about the anonymous note. I kept thinking about it all during practice, and while we were at the Monkey Jungle, too.

One of my friends has my diary. He or she could start blabbing about what I wrote any second. Then everyone will hate me forever. How awful is *that*?

Tonight, we had a pizza party on the beach. The sun was setting over the water and turning it reddish-gold. I hardly touched my conch and pineapple slice.

Everyone was buzzing about the tournament.

"The round-robin volleyball event is first," Ashley explained as she chowed down on a slice of shrimp and mango pizza. "That means the eight teams are divided into two sections."

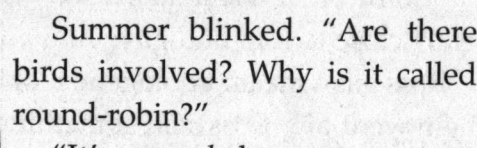

Summer blinked. "Are there birds involved? Why is it called round-robin?"

"It's *round* because we go around and around until we've played everyone in our section,"

Two for the Road

Ashley replied. "I don't know about the *robin* part. Maybe some guy named Robin invented the idea."

"Did Batman help?" Jeremy cracked up at his own joke.

"Ha-ha," Elise said.

While everyone talked, I glanced around the circle. I kept wondering who had my diary. Dana? No. She didn't join the group till late. Cheryl? Jeremy? Elise? Summer? Seth? Justin?

The person had written "Wait for my next message." When would that be happening? And what would the message say?

After dinner a bunch of people went off for a dip in the pool. Ashley wanted to take a walk on the beach and do some last-minute strategising for tomorrow.

I decided to go up to my room and sulk.

I grabbed a bunch of magazines and lay down on my bed. A balmy breeze blew through my window and stirred the curtains around. I could see a thin little sliver of a crescent moon in the sky.

I was just getting started on an article called "Do You Know Who Your Friends *Really* Are?" when I heard the sound of footsteps at my door. Quiet footsteps, as if the person didn't want to be heard.

I sat up, my heart hammering in my chest. I saw

a white envelope being slipped under the door.

I jumped out of bed and ran to the door – and flung it open.

"Ow!"

The diary thief was standing there, rubbing his head from where I'd banged him with the doorknob.

It was Jeremy!

I grabbed the envelope and ripped it open. Inside, there was a note like the one I got yesterday, with the letters cut out from a magazine. The note said:

"*You* have my diary!" I cried out.

Jeremy glanced around. "Shhhh!" he hissed.

He grabbed my arm and pushed me into my room, then he closed the door. "Quiet! Someone might hear us!" he snapped.

"Jeremy, how could you?" I said angrily. "You

Two for the Road

have to give me back my diary right now!"

"Not so fast," he said with a sly smile. "First, you have to do me some favours."

I didn't like the sound of that. "Favours? What favours?"

"First, the doughnuts. After that . . . I'll let you know."

I glared at him. "And what if I refuse?"

"Then I'm going to tell Cheryl and Ross and Seth, and everyone else what you wrote about them," Jeremy warned. "Let's see. What was my favourite? Something about *GuyStyle* magazine?"

He really *did* have my diary. Jeremy, who put a goldfish in my sippy cup when we were three. Jeremy, who taped a "Kick Me" sign on the back of my homecoming dress.

I was doomed!

"Oh, all right," I said through clenched teeth. "I'll do whatever you say."

Jeremy looked smug. "Good. We have a deal."

Could I trust him? Totally not. He could make me do all these favours and still blab about my diary to everyone.

On the other hand, did I have a choice?

Chapter 9

Sunday

Dear Diary,

The tournament is underway!

It kicked off this morning. I went down to the beach after breakfast with everyone else. Four volleyball nets had been set up. There were dozens of kids scattered around, doing warm-up stretches and laps.

Angela Velasquez got up on a little stage and held up a megaphone. "Welcome, everyone! We're about to start the round-robin competition."

"Go, Oakdale!" someone shouted.

"Okay, here's the deal," Angela went on. "The eight schools are divided into two sections. Your team captains have the section assignments. If you're in Section One, you have to play the other three teams in your section. At the end of the day we'll tally who's won the most games. May the best team win!"

The crowd cheered. I gathered my volleyball team together, and we went into a huddle. "Our first game is against Teasdale Junior High, from Maryland," I said, reading off the sheet Angela had

Two for the Road

given me. "We can beat them! Think positive! Remember why we're doing this!"

"To score free tickets to Seaquarium?" Jeremy piped up.

"To help save Florida wildlife," I corrected him. "Watch out for the tall redheaded girl with the killer serve. I saw her during practice yesterday, and she's really good. Justin, take it easy with the spikes. Dana, remember to keep your eye on the ball. Okay, good luck, everyone!"

We burst out of the huddle with a big cheer and trotted over to the volleyball net. The Teasdale team was waiting for us. They looked . . . *determined*. Well, so were we!

I took a deep breath and watched from the sidelines as my team members took their places. Angela blew the whistle to start the game.

"Go, team!" I said, pumping my fist in the air. "You can do it!"

That first game was a nail-biter. The tall redheaded girl from Teasdale really *did* have a killer serve. No one on our team could come close to it.

But we ended up winning that game, anyway. Ross, Summer, and Justin were in top form. Mary-Kate seemed a little distracted, but she played really well, too. Jeremy pulled his weight.

Two of a Kind Diaries

And best of all, Dana was on good behaviour. She didn't mess up shots or anything like that.

We lost the next game, against Immaculate Heart from Delaware – by a hair.

By the end of the day, we were ranked third among the nine teams. I asked Angela what that meant for the rest of the tournament.

"That means that for you to come in first place overall, you have to win the next two out of three events: the elimination volleyball competition tomorrow, water-skiing on Tuesday, or the bicycle race on Wednesday," she explained.

Two out of three? Hey, no problem!

I was beginning to think that we really *could* win the gold.

Dear Diary,

The nightmare has begun.

Okay, so it's great that we did so well in the round-robin competition today. But how can you enjoy the thrill of victory when your life is being ruined by a blackmailing rat . . . named Jeremy Burke?

I quickly found out what he meant by "favours." He wanted me to be his personal maid.

After the volleyball competition, he told me to

Two for the Road

fetch him a towel. And a glass of iced tea. And then a special squiggly straw for the iced tea.

He got even more carried away at dinner time. Mrs. Clare had organised a big clambake at Egret Point, down the beach from the hotel. During the clambake, Jeremy kept ordering me around: "Get me seconds, Mary-Kate." "I need another drink, Mary-Kate." "You didn't put enough butter on the corn, Mary-Kate."

Ashley was hanging out with Phoebe. At one point she noticed that I was carrying a plate of clams and potato salad over to Jeremy. She made a beeline in my direction and tapped me on the shoulder.

"Okay, I'm a little confused," Ashley said. "Why are you bringing Jeremy his food?"

"I'm just trying to be nice," I lied. "He's our cousin – a family member. What's the big deal?"

"Nice to *Jeremy*?" Ashley said incredulously. "Don't you remember the time he filled your shampoo bottle with maple syrup? Or when he sent you anonymous letters saying that you had bad breath?"

I clamped my hand over my mouth. "Is my breath okay?"

"You do *not* have bad breath," Ashley said

impatiently. "That's not the point. The point is, Jeremy has been harassing you – and me – since we were born. So why are you being nice to him?"

I shrugged.

Ashley narrowed her eyes at me. "Are you feeling okay? What is it, are you still stressed out about your missing diary?"

I grabbed her arm. "Shhh!" I hissed. "Don't even mention that!" I glanced over at Jeremy to make sure he hadn't overheard. He had said in his first note that I wasn't supposed to talk to anyone about the diary.

But he didn't seem to be paying attention. He was too busy chowing down on his clams.

He noticed me looking at him. "Yo, Mary-Kate!" he called out. Although it was hard to understand him because his mouth was full of clams. "Hurry up with that plate! And where's my lemonade? Did you forget my lemonade?"

"Oh, sorry, Jeremy, I'll be right back with that!" I replied sweetly. Was there some way I could slip a bad clam onto his plate? I wondered.

"I only have three words to say to you," Ashley said. "Are . . . you . . . nuts?"

"Just trust me," I said with a sigh. "I know what I'm doing."

Bad Clam

Chapter 10

Monday

Dear Diary,

After dinner last night Jeremy made me hand-wash his lucky socks so they would be dry in time for the elimination volleyball competition today. Then this morning he called me at the crack of dawn.

"Rise and shine!" he said when I'd picked up the phone.

"What *time* is it?" I mumbled. Across the room Ashley groaned and hid her head under the covers.

"It's time to get me breakfast," Jeremy said cheerfully. "Call room service for me, would you, M.K.? Let's see, how about three poached eggs, a side of bacon, a side of ham, a side of sausage, and a yogurt smoothie? I gotta be in top form for the volleyball competition today, so I need a lot of protein."

"Hang on." I reached over to the nightstand for a piece of paper and a pen. "You could have called room service yourself," I muttered as I scribbled his order.

"What was that, M.K.? I didn't hear you."

"Nothing."

"Oh, and hey, where are my lucky socks?"

"They're almost dry," I snapped. "Can I go now?"

Two of a Kind Diaries

"Yeah. Except, try to work on your attitude, okay? You're kind of crabby today. I don't like crabby."

"I'll work on it," I snapped, and slammed down the phone.

Ashley's head popped out from under the covers. "Who was *that*?"

"Oh, nobody. Wrong number."

Ashley glared at me suspiciously. "I'm going back to sleep now. Try not to get any more wrong numbers, okay?"

I dragged the phone into the bathroom and called room service from there, so Ashley wouldn't hear. Jeremy's lucky socks were hanging on the shower rack. I forced myself to touch them. They were dry.

Oh, Diary – what has my life come to? Maybe I should just call Jeremy's bluff and let him blab about my Last Will and Testament. Could losing all my friends be any worse than being his slave twenty-four hours a day?

Then I thought about the mean things I'd written about Cheryl and Summer and everyone else.

I realised that there was no way around it. I needed Jeremy to keep my secret . . . a secret.

I thought Jeremy might leave me alone until

Two for the Road

lunch time, but I was wrong. He had plans for me during the elimination volleyball competition.

The competition started at nine o'clock sharp. The deal was this: the top four teams from yesterday's round-robin competition would participate.

Since we came in third place yesterday, we were up. In the semi-final round, we were playing Oakdale Middle School from North Carolina. If we won that round, we would be in the finals. And if we won that, we would be the winners.

"Yo, M.K.," Jeremy called out just before we were ready to start playing Oakdale. "I need you to do me a favour."

I gritted my teeth. "What?"

"Whenever you get the ball, pass it to me, okay?" he whispered, glancing around. "I want to get lots of shots over the net."

"No way!" I cried out. "Ashley'll have a fit!"

Jeremy narrowed his eyes at me. "Okay, then. Let's see, where's Summer? I'm sure she'd be *real* interested in knowing what you left her in your will. And what about—"

"All right, all right." I glared at him. "I'll pass you the ball."

Two of a Kind Diaries

Dear Diary,

Has my sister totally lost her mind? During the game against Oakdale this morning, she kept passing the ball to Jeremy. Then *he* would get the point.

And every time Jeremy made a point, he would do this obnoxious little dance and shout, "I rule, you drool!" to the Oakdale players. That was typical Jeremy. But Mary-Kate wasn't acting like typical Mary-Kate.

I called her aside during a break. "Okay, what's up?" I snapped.

"What do you mean?" Mary-Kate said innocently.

"Why do you keep passing the ball to Cousin Dearest?"

"I'm trying to set up shots for my fellow team members instead of hogging the ball," she explained reasonably.

"Your fellow team members? You're not passing the ball to anyone but Jeremy!"

"But we're winning, aren't we?" Mary-Kate pointed out defensively.

"Just pass the ball to someone else from now on, okay?" I said. "Or hit it over the net yourself. That's an order!"

Two for the Road

Was it my imagination, or did Mary-Kate look really panic-stricken when I said that? She rushed over to Jeremy and whispered something to him. What was going on between those two?

In the end we managed to win the semi-final round against Oakdale. We were in the finals!

We had to play a really tough-looking school from Connecticut, Coate Academy. Everyone on their team was super-cut and six feet tall, even the girls. Because it was the finals, all the other schools gathered around to watch. Talk about pressure!

The score was practically tied the whole game. There was just one problem. This time it wasn't Jeremy. It was Dana who kept jumping in front of everyone else to get the ball.

I called a quick time-out and went up to Dana. "Dana," I whispered. "I really appreciate how hard you're playing. But you've got to stay in your spot and let other people have the ball once in a while."

Dana flipped her hair over her shoulders. "Why?"

"Because this is a team," I reminded her. "You've got to let your teammates get the ball sometimes."

Dana glared at me. "Whatever."

The game resumed. It was down to a single point. If Coate won the next point, they were going

Two of a Kind Diaries

to win the game – and the event. We had to hold the line.

It was Coate's serve. When the serve came, Ross fell to his knees and bobbed it over to Jeremy, who slammed it over the net. A guy on the Coate team returned it. He hadn't got a good angle on it, though, so it came back over the net at a slow, steady speed. It would be an easy shot for us.

The ball came towards Dana. All she had to do was move a little to the left. No problem, I thought.

But Dana didn't move. Not an inch. The ball fell to the ground and rolled around and around in the sand.

"We win!" someone on the Coate team shouted. "We win the competition!" The crowd broke into wild applause.

Dana turned around and looked right at me. "You told me to stay in my spot," she said with a shrug.

I realised what had happened.

She had missed the shot deliberately.

Chapter 11

Monday

Dear Diary,

I know I already wrote to you today, Diary. But I had to write to you again.

Because I am having a really, really, *really* bad day!

At dinner time I was still miffed about Dana missing that shot. I knew she did it on purpose, just to make me mad!

Well, it worked!

I decided I wasn't going to say anything to Dana about any of this. Not a word. I mean, why let her know that I care?

But then Dana came sauntering up to my table during dinner. I was sitting with Mary-Kate and Phoebe, munching down on hot dogs and spicy coleslaw.

"Hi, guys," Dana said cheerfully. She looked even more smug than usual. "Great game today, Mary-Kate. Too bad we lost!"

"Well, it was close, anyway," Mary-Kate said distractedly. She tried to squirt mustard on her hot dog and missed.

"Tomorrow *is* another day," Phoebe piped up.

"Maybe you should work on your defence, Mary-Kate," Dana suggested. "We probably would have won if you hadn't passed all those shots to Jeremy."

Mary-Kate gasped. I felt blood rushing to my cheeks. "*What*?" I cried out. "We lost because of *you*, Dana. We would have won if you hadn't missed that piece-of-cake shot in the end. On purpose!"

Dana laughed. "I did no such thing. You're the one who told me to stay in my spot!"

"That's not what I meant, and you know it!" I snapped. "Everyone saw you miss that shot. And everyone knows why you did it, too. You've been after me ever since I got voted team captain instead of you! You're just jealous!" I was so angry, my voice squeaked on those last few words.

As luck would have it, Ross had overheard this entire conversation from the next table. He stood up and came over and frowned at me.

"Ashley, aren't you being kind of unfair?" Ross demanded. "You can't blame Dana just because we lost today. It happens."

Dana squeezed his hand. "Oh, thank you, Ross." She sniffed. "I really appreciate your support."

Two for the Road

She reached up and pretended to wipe some tears from her eyes.

What a phony!

"But, Ross—" I protested.

"I mean, you can't beat up on a team member for missing one little crummy shot," Ross went on.

I had heard enough. I scooted back my chair and rose to my feet. "You don't know how wrong you are," I burst out at Ross. "You two deserve each other!" And with that, I ran out of the dining room, trying not to let anyone see that *I* was the one with real tears in my eyes.

Dear Diary,

Poor Ashley! At dinner she and Dana had a huge fight about the volleyball competition. Ross got in the middle of it, and Dana somehow managed to get him to take her side. Ashley was so upset, she went running out of there.

I got up and started to chase after her. But guess who stopped me?

"Oh, Mary-Kaaaaate!" Jeremy called over from his table. "I need you to do me a favour."

"Not now, Jeremy," I replied, speed-walking to the door. "Ashley needs me!"

Two of a Kind Diaries

"Well, *I* need you more," he said, narrowing his eyes. "Have you forgotten about our little deal?"

I forced myself to do a U-turn and go over to his table. "*What*? What do you want?" I said, clenching my fists.

"I'm having a hard time playing Viper III and eating dinner at the same time," Jeremy explained, pointing to his GameMan. "I need you to feed me my hot dog so I can keep playing."

"No way!"

"I don't think 'no' is an option. Do you, M.K.?"

I gritted my teeth and sat down next to him. I picked up his hot dog and held it up to his mouth.

Elise, Cheryl, and Summer were watching me from the next table. Elise whispered something to Cheryl and Summer, and they all started giggling.

"Put more relish on that first, Mary-Kate," Jeremy ordered. He pressed a couple of buttons on his GameMan. "Come on, die, you viper!"

This is what humiliation is, I thought. *Hand-feeding hot dogs to Jeremy while all your friends watch.*

I had definitely hit rock bottom. It was time for drastic measures.

Chapter 12

Wednesday

Dear Diary,

When I woke up this morning, the first thing I thought was: *at least Dana isn't on the water-skiing team. So she can't mess up the water-skiing competition today.*

Well, guess what, Diary? I was totally wrong!

The water-skiing competition is divided into three parts: jumps, tricks, and the slalom course. After breakfast, about ten minutes before the jumps portion was set to begin, Summer came running up to me on the beach. She looked all panicky.

"Bad news!" she announced.

"You broke a nail," I teased her.

"I did?" Summer held up her nails and studied them.

"No, no, I was just joking . . . What's up, Summer?"

"Cheryl just fell down the stairs and sprained her wrist!" she announced.

"What?" I cried out. "Is she okay?"

"Her wrist's all black and blue and yucky," Summer replied, making a face. "Mrs. Clare is taking her to the doctor."

My mind was racing. Cheryl was on the water-skiing team. Without her, we were one team member short. I had to replace her ASAP.

I checked off my options in my head. The water-skiing team consisted of Devon, Mary-Kate, Summer, Jeremy, and me. I tried to remember what had happened during the water-skiing tryouts last Thursday.

Oh, yeah.

Oh, NO!

The only other person who even knew how to water-ski was . . . Dana!

Not only was she a pretty mediocre water-skier, but she was on a mission to make my life miserable!

Dana was incredibly smug when I asked her to fill in for Cheryl. "Oh, so *now* you're begging me to be on the water-skiing team," she said.

I had to bite my lip to keep from saying anything.

"Go ahead, beg," she insisted.

I took a deep breath and counted to ten. Think of the team, I told myself. Think of the manatees. Think of all the money that's going to go towards saving Florida wildlife. "Please, Dana," I forced myself to say in a sweet, pleading voice. "We

Two for the Road

really need you on the water-skiing team. Okay?"

Dana tossed her hair over her shoulders. "Oh, okay. If you put it that way." She rushed off to change into her bathing suit.

While we were all waiting for her to come back, Devon marched up to me. "What's going on? I heard Cheryl was out."

"Dana's taking her place," I told him.

I must have looked pretty unhappy, because Devon said, "What's the matter? She knows how to water-ski, right?"

"Sort of."

"Then what's the problem?"

I told him what the problem was. I told him that I was afraid she'd sabotage the water-skiing competition, just like she'd done with the volleyball competition yesterday.

When I was finished, Devon nodded. "Don't worry – I'll take care of it."

"You'll take care of it? How?" I demanded.

"Just leave it to me."

Dana came back a few minutes later, dressed in a black tank suit. "Okay, surf's up or whatever. I'm ready!" she announced.

"Hey, Dana," Devon said, grinning widely at her. "I'll make you a bet."

Two of a Kind Diaries

Dana's eyes flashed. "Bet? What bet?"

"I bet I can beat you in jumps, tricks, *and* slalom," Devon said.

"Oh, no way!" Dana laughed and shook her head. "I'm going to beat *you*, hands down. Just you watch. What are we betting?"

"Loser has to buy the winner the new 4-You CD."

I stifled a gasp. Devon didn't even *like* 4-You!

"Oooh, I don't have that yet!" Dana exclaimed. "You're on!"

Devon flashed me a smile as we picked up our water skis and headed off to join the other schools. I smiled back at him. Who cared if he didn't like 4-You or mint chocolate-chip ice cream? For today, anyway, he was my hero!

Dear Diary,

Guess what? We came in first place in the water-skiing competition! White Oak and Harrington rule!

The entire team pulled off stellar performances at jumps, tricks, and slalom. Even Dana was in top form. I wonder what got into her? She was acting like Queen of the Waves.

Ashley was soooo psyched. She said that all we have to do now is win the 10K bike race tomorrow.

Two for the Road

If we can pull that off, we'll place first overall – and we'll get to go to Seaquarium!

I was pretty psyched about our big victory today, too. Until Jeremy came up to me and handed me his water skis and yucky, drippy wetsuit.

"Carry these for me, M.K.," he commanded. "I'm going to go to the hotel gift shop to pick out some postcards. Why don't you meet me in my room in, say . . . fifteen minutes? I'll need you to take dictation."

"Dictation?" I repeated dumbly. "What for?"

"Postcards," Jeremy replied. "Mom and Dad get really annoyed if I don't write to them once a day. I'll dictate, and you can write down what I say."

I gritted my teeth. "Fine."

I dropped Jeremy's water skis and wetsuit off in the locker room area, then went up to his room. I was about to knock when Justin opened the door. He and Jeremy were roommates on this trip.

He smiled at me. "Hey, what's up?"

"Is Jeremy here?" I asked him.

"No, but you can wait for him," Justin said. "I'm going down to the lobby to get some soda. You want anything?"

"No, thanks."

Two of a Kind Diaries

Justin took off down the hall. I went inside their room and shut the door.

Right then I realised how I was going to get out of my horrible, terrible dilemma.

Without wasting another minute I started rifling through Jeremy's stuff. "Okay, Diary, where are you?" I said to myself.

He had to be hiding it somewhere. And if I could just get my hands on it, I would be home free! Jeremy couldn't blackmail me anymore. He could still *tell* people what I wrote, but without the diary, he wouldn't have any proof. No one would ever believe him!

I dug through his suitcase, his backpack, his dirty laundry. I searched under his bed, through his dressing table drawers, and in every nook and cranny.

There was no sign of my diary anywhere.

I was just about to give up when I felt something under Jeremy's pillow. I pulled it out. It was a diary!

But it wasn't *my* diary. On the cover, it said: JEREMY BURKE'S EXCELLENT DIARY.

Holy cow! I thought, grinning from ear to ear. *Maybe THIS is my ticket to freedom!*

Chapter 13

Thursday

Dear Diary,

I woke up this morning in a cold sweat.

This was the day. This was the day we were going to have to win the 10K.

Sunlight streamed through our curtains. Mary-Kate was still asleep. She was snoring and mumbling under the covers.

I went over to her bed and tapped her on the shoulder. "Hey, Mary-Kate. Wake up!"

"Hmmm? Jeremy? Your socks are almost dry. What do you want, scrambled eggs or sunny-side-up? Let me just sleep for a second. . . ."

I shook Mary-Kate harder. "Mary-Kate, wake up! You're having a bad dream."

Mary-Kate's eyes flew open. "What? Oh, hey, Ashley. Is it morning?"

"Uh-huh." I stared at my sister. "Okay, I can't stand it anymore. 'Fess up. *What* is going on with you and Jeremy?"

Mary-Kate looked scared. "What do you mean?"

"I mean, you've been acting totally bizarre for the last few days. You bring him all his meals, you hand-feed him hot dogs, and you're doing his laun-

Two of a Kind Diaries

dry. Not to mention the fact that you set up all those shots for him in volleyball, and you carried his water-skiing stuff. What's up?"

Mary-Kate sighed miserably. "Okay, I'll tell you. But you have to promise not to tell anyone – especially Jeremy!"

I held up my right hand. "I swear. Twin's honour."

Mary-Kate sighed again. "When Phoebe and I were stranded in the swamp, we were kind of thinking that we might not make it back," she explained. "So we wrote this thing in my diary called the Last Will and Testament. We left stuff for all our friends."

"That's kind of depressing," I remarked.

"Well, a lot of it was a joke. We left all kinds of *mean* stuff for our friends. And we wrote mean things about them." She paused. "Anyway, remember when I told you that I lost my diary somewhere between Camp Coral Reef and here?"

"Uh-huh."

"It turned out that Jeremy had it! And he's been blackmailing me!"

I gasped.

"He said he'd tell all my friends what I wrote about them unless I did whatever he asked," Mary-Kate went on.

I rolled my eyes. "Oh, brother. That explains a lot!"

Two for the Road

Mary-Kate's eyes gleamed. "The thing is, I found his diary. I'm going to use it to get *my* diary back."

"Way to go, sis!" I grinned.

I think Mary-Kate felt a lot better telling me all this. I gave her a hug and told her everything was going to be fine. She was never going to have to be Jeremy's personal maid again.

But at the moment I had to get ready for the big 10K!

I put on my bike shorts and top and headed downstairs. After a quick breakfast I went out to the starting line. While I was doing my stretches, the rest of my team showed up: Phoebe, Ross, Dana, Elise, and Seth.

I thought I saw Ross sneak a look at me. Was it my new SAVE THE MANATEES tank top? Or my amazing leadership skills? Either way, my heart did a little dance. But then Dana came up and pulled him off to look at her bicycle tyres.

Maybe Ross was ready to be friendly again. But now was not the time to think about this. I had to concentrate on the race.

The other schools were starting to gather around. Angela announced over the megaphone that the race would be starting in a few minutes.

Two of a Kind Diaries

I got my team into a huddle and gave everyone a pep talk.

"Okay, if we win this one, we'll get the big prize!" I cried out. "Let's go! We can do it!"

Everyone joined hands and then burst out of the huddle with a big cheer. We strapped on our helmets, straddled our bikes, and rode over to the starting line.

"On your marks, get set . . . GO!" Angela blew the whistle. The race was starting! We all squeezed our handlebars and tucked our heads and rode into the wind.

A salty breeze whipped my hair around. I could hear chains clanking and wheels turning all around me. I tried not to get psyched out by the fact that there were so many kids riding next to me, behind me, and in front of me. I just tried to focus on pumping my legs as hard as I could.

The course took us up the beach, through a big park, and back again. People cheered all along the way. Seagulls swooped through the air.

By the 9K mark, Phoebe, Ross, Elise, and Seth were way up front, along with half a dozen kids from other schools. I was somewhere in the middle. Dana

Two for the Road

was lagging behind. Was she doing it on purpose? I pedalled extra-hard, trying to shave every extra second off my time so I could make up for Dana. At the end of the race the team with the lowest combined score would win.

I saw the finish line up ahead. Almost there!

And then my front tyre hit a rock.

My bike jerked violently. I wasn't prepared. The next thing I knew, I flew into the air and landed on the pavement, hard.

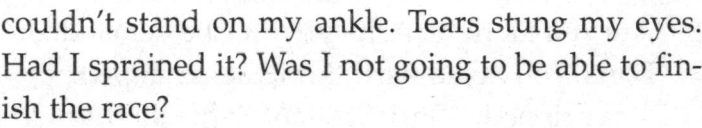

I heard other bikes whizzing past me. I tried to get up, but I couldn't stand on my ankle. Tears stung my eyes. Had I sprained it? Was I not going to be able to finish the race?

A bike screeched to a halt in front of me. I looked up and saw Dana turning around. She hesitated a moment, as if she were trying to decide what to do.

She got off her bike and ran over. "Ashley, are you okay?"

"It-it's my ankle," I told her. "I-I think it might be sprained."

"Try to stand up," she said.

She held my hand and helped me to my feet.

Two of a Kind Diaries

I put some weight on the bad ankle. It hurt, but it wasn't excruciating.

"You think you can finish?" Dana asked me.

"I'm not sure."

She flipped her hair over her shoulders. "Come on, I'll help you."

She put her arm around me and got me back up on my bike. "Easy now," she said. "Pedal with your good foot. Let the other one just kind of rest."

I did what she said. She rode beside me for the last fifteen yards.

And just like that, Dana and I crossed the finish line – side by side.

The rest of our team came running to us.

"Are you all right, Ashley?" Phoebe demanded.

"Dana, you saved her!" Summer exclaimed.

Dana grinned. "Oh, it was nothing. I do stuff like that all the time."

I could tell Dana liked being the centre of attention. She *always* liked being the centre of attention. But who was I to hold it against her? She really did save me.

And, as it turned out, she saved the race!

When the last cyclists had crossed the finish line, Angela figured out everyone's times. "The White Oak-Harrington team is the winner of the 10K!" she

Two for the Road

announced. "That also means that they win the tournament!"

Ross, Phoebe, Seth, Elise, Dana, and I screamed and grabbed one another in a big group hug. Mary-Kate, Cheryl, and everyone else came running up to us and joined the group hug, too. "We did it! We did it!" we all shouted.

My ankle still hurt, but my heart was pounding with happiness. Seaquarium, here we come! And I owed it all to Dana. Can you believe it, Diary?

Dear Diary,

Guess what? I was getting ready for the big victory party on the beach. I wanted to wear my favourite pink earrings, the ones with the crystal hearts dangling from them. Ashley gave them to me for my birthday last year.

I couldn't find one of them, though. I searched everywhere. But no earring.

I decided to check my suitcase. I ran my hand all over the lining, in case the earring had fallen into a crack or something.

Sure enough, there was the earring. And guess what else I found?

My diary!

Two of a Kind Diaries

It had somehow slipped through a tear in the lining and lodged itself way deep. I was so relieved . . .

And then I was *furious*!

Because this meant that Jeremy never had my diary to begin with! He made it all up, just so he could blackmail me into being his personal maid.

My mind was racing. On Wednesday, when everyone was hanging out at the pool, I complained to Phoebe about the missing diary. While we were talking, I thought I heard something – or someone – in the bushes. It must have been Jeremy, eavesdropping on us!

It took him less than forty-eight hours to figure out what to do with the info. On Friday he left me the first note.

I stared out of the window at the beach, where Angela and Mrs. Clare were starting a bonfire for the victory party.

"All right, Jeremy," I said, rubbing my hands together. "It's payback time!"

Chapter 14

Thursday

Dear Diary,

Life is good. No, I take that back, Diary. Life is totally, completely awesome!

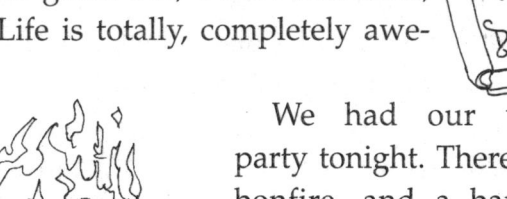

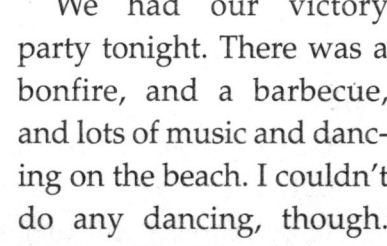

We had our victory party tonight. There was a bonfire, and a barbecue, and lots of music and dancing on the beach. I couldn't do any dancing, though. My ankle was all taped up – just like Cheryl's wrist.

"I guess we're the two casualties," Cheryl said.

"But it was worth it! We won!" Cheryl and I laughed and exchanged high fives on that.

Just then, Ross came up to us. I stopped in the middle of my high five and glanced at him in surprise. "Hey."

"Hey, Ashley." He sat down beside me on my beach blanket. Cheryl mumbled something about having to grab some dessert, then scurried away.

"How's it going?" I asked him.

Ross shrugged. "Okay."

He looked like he wanted to say something. I smiled at him and waited.

Two of a Kind Diaries

"So, listen," Ross said after a minute. "I know everyone thinks Dana's a big hero because she saved you and all that." He hesitated. "But I just wanted to tell you *you're* the real hero. You were a great team captain. Without you we probably wouldn't have won first place."

I could feel myself blushing. And smiling. And blushing some more. "Thanks, Ross," I said.

"You're welcome," Ross said. "How's your ankle?"

"Better. It wasn't a really bad sprain."

"Let me see."

He bent down and took my ankle in his hands. He peeked under the Ace bandage. "Doesn't look too bad."

His hands on my ankle were making it hard for me to think straight. Or talk. At that moment my entire vocabulary had disappeared from my brain.

Ross let go of my ankle and gazed into my eyes. "Ashley, I've missed you . . ." he began.

"I've missed you, too," I blurted out.

He reached over and gave me a hug. My heart totally melted. Ross and I were a couple again!

We spent the rest of the evening holding hands and talking.

Two for the Road

We had so much to catch up on. We even slow-danced to one song, with me hobbling on my bad ankle.

Didn't I tell you life was totally, completely awesome, Diary?

Dear Diary (my *real* diary),

Jeremy didn't know what hit him.

During the victory party, I kept messing up his orders.

"M.K., I told you to get me ginger ale, not punch," Jeremy snapped.

"What? Oh. Sorry 'bout that, Jeremy."

"And where are my barbecued ribs?"

"Hmmmm? In a minute, okay? I'm busy."

After an hour of this, Jeremy called me aside. "What's going on?" he demanded. "If you don't shape up, you know what's going to happen. I'm going to read your diary out loud, right here and now!"

"I'm sorry," I said innocently. "It won't happen again."

While we were all chowing down on toasted marshmallows, Ashley hobbled up to the front of the crowd with Angela's megaphone.

"Speech!" Seth and Justin yelled. Everyone broke into applause.

Two of a Kind Diaries

Ashley grinned and waved. "I just wanted to thank you all for being such an awesome team," she said.

More applause.

"Because of your hard work and dedication, our sponsors are donating a thousand dollars to the Wildlife Fund," Ashley went on. "Plus, we get to go to Seaquarium tomorrow and hang out with dolphins and manatees!"

Everyone cheered.

"That's all. Anyone else want to make a speech?" Ashley smiled and waved the megaphone around. Ross took it and got up to thank Mrs. Clare.

I quietly pulled Jeremy's diary out of my backpack. I opened it to the middle and leaned over to Jeremy.

"What do you think, Jer? Should I go up there and read everyone a page from your excellent diary?" I whispered. "Listen, here's a good one. 'Dear Diary. I think I'm over my stupid crush on Dana Woletsky. But maybe not. Do you think I should ask her to the Homecoming Dance, Diary? She might hold it against me that I'm Ashley and Mary-Kate's cousin. On the other hand, I could wear my lucky socks when I ask her. That might give me an edge.'"

Two for the Road

Jeremy lunged at me. "Give me that!"

"You never *did* have my diary, did you?" I said. "You're lucky I didn't just give your diary to Phoebe! She could have published it in the *Acorn*!"

Jeremy grabbed his diary from me and stomped off. His face was as red as a lobster.

Justice. It was a good feeling.

Chapter 15

Saturday

Dear Diary,

Today we went to the Seaquarium. Diary, it was amazing!

There were all kinds of awesome fish there, including tropical fish of every colour of the rainbow. We got to see sharks being fed. We saw stingrays and barracudas, too. We even got to touch a bunch of stuff, including starfish, sea cucumbers, and hermit crabs! Super-slimy!

The twelve of us, plus Mrs. Clare, were given VIP treatment. A special tour guide, Tico, took us all around. He showed us a special film about Florida ecology. He told us all kinds of cool stories about the different sea creatures.

Ross stayed by my side the whole time. We held hands and talked about the rest of the summer.

"I'll miss you," he told me.

"I'll miss you, too," I told him. "Let's e-mail each other every day!"

"Definitely! And I'll see if my parents will let me visit my cousin in Chicago," Ross promised.

My heart skipped a beat. "That would be great."

At the end of the day we got to put on our swimming suits and splash around in the pool with the

Two for the Road

dolphins. There was a whole family of them. One of them even kissed me on the nose!

The best part was when we got to meet the baby manatee! It was soft and brown and had a sweet face, kind of like a walrus's. Its mom was huge and kept nudging the baby under the water. But the baby kept popping up and blinking at us with its big brown eyes.

Our tour guide, Tico, turned to us. "So what do you think you all want to name it?" he asked us. "That's part of your prize!"

"How about Emily Dickinson?" Phoebe suggested. Emily Dickinson was Phoebe's favourite poet.

"How about Fluffy?" Summer said.

"How about Dana?" Dana said.

I raised my hand. "How about Victory?"

Everyone liked that. "Victory it is," Tico said. He smiled at the baby manatee. "Hey, Victory, welcome to the world!"

Victory blinked at us and splashed around in the water. I squeezed Ross's hand. This was the best summer vacation ever!

Two of a Kind Diaries

Dear New Diary,

Last night I decided to throw the Last Will and Testament pages from my diary in the bonfire. They were too dangerous to keep around.

Now I'm writing in my new diary. It was time for a fresh start! It's a cool-looking notebook I got today at Seaquarium, with a picture of manatees on the cover.

What lesson did I learn from all this? Never write mean stuff about your friends. Even if your diary doesn't end up disappearing.

Ashley's across the room, packing her suitcase. She looks annoyed because she can't cram everything in. I guess she bought too many souvenirs!

We're leaving first thing tomorrow for Miami airport. And then it's home to Chicago, and Dad, and all our friends there. I can't wait!

I'm going to miss Miami and the manatees. I'm also going to miss all our friends. We won't see each other for the rest of the summer.

But then we'll all be back together this fall when school starts again. I wonder what the new year will be like? After what we've been through these last four weeks in Florida, New Hampshire's going to seem pretty tame.

Or will it?

PSST! Take a sneak peek at

Dear Diary,

Aloha! That's how you say hello in Hawaiian. In a few minutes our plane will be landing at the airport in Hilo, Hawaii!

It's the first week of summer vacation and I'm on a school trip with some of my classmates from the White Oak Academy for Girls. White Oak is the boarding school in New Hampshire that I go to with my twin sister, Ashley. We're First Formers there (that means seventh-graders).

I can see long beaches and tall palm trees from the window of the plane. They're totally different from the green hills of New Hampshire. This trip is going to be awesome. Lots of my friends are here!

First there's Ashley's roommate, Phoebe Cahill, and

my roommate and best bud, Campbell Smith (who's sitting next to me). There's also Julia Langstrom, Summer Sorenson and Elise Van Hook.

Dana Woletsky is here, too. I kind of wish she *wasn't* here. She's a superpopular First Former and she's never been nice to Ashley or me. I hope I won't have to spend time with her on this trip!

Our group isn't just all girls. The Harrington School for Boys is down the road from White Oak, and they sent some of the guys to Hawaii, too! Grant Marino, Hans Jensen, Seth Samuels and Devon Benjamin all came along. And I can't forget my cousin-dearest, Jeremy. He is so annoying! Diary, the only thing Ashley and I have in common with Jeremy is a last name.

"Hey, Mary-Kate," Jeremy said, walking up the aisle. "Hold this for a second, will you?"

I held out my hand. "Eeek!" I shrieked when he dropped something wiggly in my palm. Then I realised it was only a rubber spider.

Jeremy slapped his leg. "Ha! Gets 'em every time."

I threw the spider back at Jeremy. I hope he doesn't play practical jokes the whole time we're here. This trip is going to be a real challenge and practical jokes are the last thing we need!

We're going to Hawaii for four whole weeks. For

the first half of our vacation we're participating in Wild Hawaii – a once-in-a-lifetime wilderness adventure, where we live off the land for twelve whole days. Imagine it, Diary – gathering food, building shelter, surviving on our own! Wow, it sounds even cooler now than when Ashley read me the description from the brochure!

For the second half of our vacation, we're off to an island resort, where our only responsibilities will be to relax and have fun!

Campbell elbowed me. "Did you know that certain kinds of flowers are edible?" she said. She was reading from a book called *The Outdoor Survival Guide*. Before we left for vacation, Campbell and I had gone to the school library to take out books on camping in Hawaii. We wanted to make sure we were ready for anything!

I shook my head. "Nope. What else have you learned?"

Campbell jabbed her finger at another page. "That you can use the leaves of the aloe plant to treat minor burns and cuts."

I took a sip of the pineapple juice that the flight attendant had passed out. "Excellent! We'll totally be able to use all that information. Can I look through the books tonight?"

Campbell grinned. "Sure. After we finish reading these, we'll be experts at living in the wild."

It's a little scary to think that we'll be living the way people did zillions of years ago, without electricity and Ben and Jerry's ice cream. (Just kidding about the ice cream, Diary.) But we'll have a Wild Hawaii guide to tell us what to do and to take us to cool places on the island. I can't wait!

"Ms. Clare, will there be someone to carry our suitcases at the airport?" Summer asked from across the aisle.

Ms. Clare is the assistant headmistress of White Oak. She's really nice. Mr. Turnbull, the assistant headmaster of Harrington, is here, too. When we first met him, he was really mean and scary – but these days he's much more laid-back. Right now he's sitting a few rows in front of me trying to play the ukulele!

"Why do you ask?" Ms. Clare replied.

Summer flipped her long blonde hair over her shoulders. "Because I brought, like, five or six suitcases."

Elise gasped. "Summer, Ms. Clare told us to pack *light*!"

Summer shrugged. "I thought I *was* packing light. Five suitcases isn't a lot of clothing."

Dana leaned across Summer and flashed me a smile. "Speaking of clothing, that is such a cute sundress, Mary-Kate!"

"Um, thanks," I said slowly. *Dana giving me a compliment? Unbelievable*, I thought.

"It really hides those extra pounds," she added.

I took a deep breath and counted to ten. I didn't want to say anything that would get me in trouble.

"Mary-Kate! Smile and say something for the camera!"

I glanced up. Phoebe's head popped over the seat in front of me. She was holding a video camera. I could tell by the blinking red light near the lens that she was recording.

"Hey, everyone!" I said with a big wave. "Wish you were here!"

Phoebe has the coolest job on this vacation. She will be camping on the beach with us, but she's not part of the Wild Hawaii challenge. She's here to capture all the action on video. The footage will be shown at a special school assembly this autumn. (I hope she doesn't catch me doing anything stupid!)

"Attention, passengers," the pilot announced over the loudspeaker. "Please fasten your seat belts."

Yay! We're almost ready to land. Hello, Hilo!

PSST! Take a sneak peek
at

Surf, Sand, and Secrets

Dear Diary,

Oops! Sorry about that. I didn't mean for you to get splashed. I've never written in you while I was on a yacht before. Actually, I've never even *been* on a yacht before! It's so cool!

A group of us from the White Oak Academy for Girls are here on a special school trip. That includes my sister, Mary-Kate, and a bunch of our friends from our class from the First Form. Diary, I'll never understand why they don't just call it the seventh grade. Oh, well . . .

A few of the boys from our brother school, Harrington, are here with us, including my weird and annoying cousin Jeremy Burke. Right now he's trying to catch fish off the back of the yacht.

He said he couldn't wait for lunch.

I'm sitting at a table on the top deck, so I have a perfect view of everything. We're cruising through Hanalei Bay near the island of Kauai. That's one of the islands of Hawaii. We're on our way to Part Two of our summer vacation at the Hanalei Beach Resort!

Part One was spent in Hilo, which is on a different Hawaiian island. We played a survival game called Wild Hawaii, in which we had to live on the beach for twelve whole days.

Well, maybe not twelve days for me. I kind of got booted from Wild Hawaii on the very first day for not following the rules. Luckily my friends Elise Van Hook and Summer Sorenson got kicked out (accidentally on purpose) right after I did.

"I love this yacht!" my roommate, Phoebe Cahill, cried. She was sitting next to me and filming Elise and Summer, who were leaning against the ship's rail and waving.

Phoebe's been recording our whole trip. She says it's good experience since her dream is to be a journalist.

"Pssst. Ashley."

I glanced up. Dana Woletsky was leaning toward me from the next table. *This can't be good,* I thought.

Dana isn't what I would call "a nice person."

"I was just thinking about the juicy secret I know about you," Dana said with a smirk.

I had no idea what Dana was talking about, but I could feel my cheeks turning red anyway. "What secret?" I asked.

"Don't worry," Dana said. "You'll find out soon enough." Her smirk turned into a big smile. "And you're going to get in so much trouble. I can't wait!" She tossed her shiny dark hair and turned back around to her own table.

I wasn't sure if Dana *really* knew a secret about me. You can never tell with her. Maybe she was just saying that so I'd be worried for the rest of the trip.

I think she's still angry that I won a hundred-dollar shopping spree in Hilo. You see, Diary, I volunteered at Wild Hawaii to help with chores even after I got kicked out. Our guide was so impressed he gave me a prize for teamwork!

Well, I'm not going to have time to worry about Dana. There's too much fun planned!

"Ashley, want to check out the resort's brochure?" Mary-Kate pulled a chair up to our table. She gave me a little smile, but I could tell that she wasn't exactly happy. She's bummed because she and her best friend, Campbell Smith, had a fight in Hilo. I hope they make up soon.

"Sure," I said, taking the booklet.

Phoebe leaned over my shoulder. "Look!" she said. "They have hula dancing! Hey, maybe I'll get to wear a grass skirt – just like Elvis Presley in my favorite movie, *Blue Hawaii*."

I giggled. Phoebe loved old movies. In fact, she loved anything vintage. At the moment she was wearing an orange 1950s bathing suit with a big yellow flower on one shoulder.

Elise brushed back her long brown hair. "Well, I can't wait to go surfing," she piped up.

"I'm already an expert surfer," Hans Jensen called over from the next table. Hans is good at almost every sport. He lets everyone know it, too.

"I can't wait to try wave running," Mary-Kate said.

I smiled. "I'm going to try *all* those things," I said. "This is going to be an awesome week."

I looked at Summer, who was now sitting next to Hans. "Summer, what are you going to do first?"

But Summer didn't seem to hear me. She had her head buried in a magazine.

"Earth to Summer. Come in, Summer," I joked.

"Huh?" Summer's blonde head snapped up.

"What are you reading?" I asked.

Summer held up the latest issue of *The National*

Inquisitor. "I am so freaked out. There's the creepiest article in here."

"What's it about?" Mary-Kate asked.

"Aliens," Summer said. She leaned forward. "It says that just last week aliens were spotted hovering over Kauai. That's the island our resort is on!"

She pointed to a fuzzy picture of something that looked like a lit-up spaceship. It was hovering over a few palm trees. The headline read ALOHA, ALIENS!

A bunch of kids gathered around to look at the picture.

"Whoa," Julia Langstrom said.

"Cool!" Grant Marino added.

I rolled my eyes. They didn't really believe in this stuff, did they? I mean, the picture was a total fake.

"It says here that the aliens left a trail of purple shells along the beach," Summer added in a hushed voice. "And the trail pointed straight towards"– she gulped – "the Hanalei Beach Resort!"

I almost burst out laughing. What a joke!

"Hey, my cousin saw a spaceship when he was on vacation in Nevada," Seth Samuels said.

"Really? What did it look like?" Phoebe asked, putting down her video camera. She actually looked interested.

I frowned at my roommate. Why was she even

asking something like that? Maybe she was just playing along. Or maybe it was because she was a journalist – always asking questions.

"It was spinning around and had lots of blinking lights," Seth replied. "You know. The usual."

Summer nodded seriously. "We see aliens back home in California all the time." She shuddered. "My friend's brother's surfing buddy almost got abducted once. They tried to take him right out of the water."

Everyone gasped.

"How can you guys believe in UFOs?" I asked.

Summer stared at me. "Ashley, the proof is right in front of your eyes!" She tapped a hot-pink fingernail at the article.

"Whatever you say, Summer." I sat back and folded my arms. "But I'm telling you. There's no such thing as aliens."

mary-kateandashley

(1)	It's a Twin Thing	(0 00 714480 6)
(2)	How to Flunk Your First Date	(0 00 714479 2)
(3)	The Sleepover Secret	(0 00 714478 4)
(4)	One Twin Too Many	(0 00 714477 6)
(5)	To Snoop or Not to Snoop	(0 00 714476 8)
(6)	My Sister the Supermodel	(0 00 714475 X)
(7)	Two's a Crowd	(0 00 714474 1)
(8)	Let's Party	(0 00 714473 3)
(9)	Calling All Boys	(0 00 714472 5)
(10)	Winner Take All	(0 00 714471 7)
(11)	PS Wish You Were Here	(0 00 714470 9)
(12)	The Cool Club	(0 00 714469 5)
(13)	War of the Wardrobes	(0 00 714468 7)
(14)	Bye-Bye Boyfriend	(0 00 714467 9)
(15)	It's Snow Problem	(0 00 714466 0)

HarperCollins*Entertainment*

TM & © 2002 Dualstar Entertainment Group, LLC.

mary-kateandashley

- (16) Likes Me, Likes Me Not (0 00 714465 2)
- (17) Shore Thing (0 00 714464 4)
- (18) Two for the Road (0 00 714463 6)
- (19) Surprise, Surprise! (0 00 714462 8)
- (20) Sealed with a Kiss (0 00 714461 X)
- (21) Now you see him, Now you don't (0 00 714446 6)
- (22) April-Fool's Rules (0 00 714460 1)
- (23) Island Girls (0 00 714445 8)
- (24) Surf Sand and Secrets (0 00 714459 8)
- (25) Closer Than Ever (0 00 715881 5)
- (26) The Perfect Gift (0 00 715882 3)
- (27) The Facts About Flirting (0 00 715883 1)

HarperCollins*Entertainment*

TM & © 2002 Dualstar Entertainment Group, LLC.

mary-kateandashley

Meet Chloe and Riley Carlson.
So much to do...
so little time

(1)	How to Train a Boy	(0 00 714458 X)		
(2)	Instant Boyfriend	(0 00 714448 2)	(8) The Love Factor	(0 00 714454 7)
(3)	Too Good to be True	(0 00 714449 0)	(9) Dating Game	(0 00 714447 4)
(4)	Just Between Us	(0 00 714450 4)	*Coming Soon...*	
(5)	Tell Me About It	(0 00 714451 2)	(10) A Girl's Guide to Guys	(0 00 714455 5)
(6)	Secret Crush	(0 00 714452 0)	(11) Boy Crazy	(0 00 714456 3)
(7)	Girl Talk	(0 00 714453 9)	(12) Best Friends Forever	(0 00 714457 1)

HarperCollins*Entertainment*

PARACHUTE PRESS   DUALSTAR PUBLICATIONS   mary-kateandashley.com AOL Keyword: mary-kateandashley

TM & © 2002 Dualstar Entertainment Group, LLC.

mary-kateandashley
Sweet 16

(1) *Never Been Kissed*   (0 00 714879 8)
(2) *Wishes and Dreams*   (0 00 714880 1)
(3) *The Perfect Summer*   (0 00 714881 X)

HarperCollins*Entertainment*

TM & © 2002 Dualstar Entertainment Group, LLC.

Mary-Kate and Ashley get their first jobs ...in Rome!

Out on video and DVD 3 November*

*date correct at time of going to print

mary-kateandashley.com
AOL Keyword: mary-kateandashley

Distributed by

Mary-Kate and Ashley's latest exciting movie adventure

Available to own on video and DVD 29th July 2002

mary-kateandashley.com
AOL Keyword: mary-kateandashley

Real Books for Real Girls

b the 1st 2 kno mary-kateandashley

It's What YOU Read

REGISTER 4 THE HARPERCOLLINS AND MK&ASH TEXT CLUB AND KEEP UP2 D8 WITH THE L8EST MK&ASH BOOK NEWS AND MORE.

SIMPLY TEXT TOK, FOLLOWED BY YOUR GENDER (M/F), DATE OF BIRTH (DD/MM/YY) AND POSTCODE TO: 07786277301.

SO, IF YOU ARE A GIRL BORN ON THE 12TH MARCH 1986 AND LIVE IN THE POSTCODE DISTRICT RG19 YOUR MESSAGE WOULD LOOK LIKE THIS: TOKF120386RG19.

IF YOU ARE UNDER 14 YEARS WE WILL NEED YOUR PARENTS' OR GUARDIANS' PERMISSION FOR US TO CONTACT YOU. PLEASE ADD THE LETTER 'G' TO THE END OF YOUR MESSAGE TO SHOW YOU HAVE YOUR PARENTS' CONSENT. LIKE THIS: TOKF120386RG19G.

Terms and conditions:
By sending a text message you agree to receive further text messages and exciting book offers from HarperCollins, publishers of Mary-Kate and Ashley and other children's books. You can unsubscribe at any time by texting 'STOP' to the number advertised. All text messages are charged at standard rate - maximum cost 12p. Promoter: HarperCollins.

HarperCollins*Entertainment*

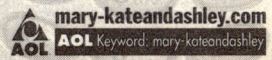

TM & © 2002 Dualstar Entertainment Group, Inc.

the mary-kateandashley brand

Fab freebie!

You can have loads of fun with this ultra-cool Glistening Stix from the **mary-kateandashley** brand. Great glam looks for eyes, lips – or anywhere else you fancy!

you have to do is **collect four tokens from four different books from the mary-kateandashley brand** (no photocopies, please!), send them to us with your address on the coupon below – and a groovy Glistening Stix will be on its way to you!

Go on, get collecting and sparkle like a star!

Real Books for Real Girls

It's What **YOU** Read

TOKEN

Name: ....

Address: ....

....

e-mail: ....

☐ Tick here if you do not wish to receive further information about children's books.

Send coupon to: **mary-kateandashley Marketing**, HarperCollins Publishers, 77-85 Fulham Palace Road, Hammersmith, London W6 8JB.

Terms and conditions: proof of sending cannot be considered proof of receipt. Not redeemable for cash. 28 days delivery. Offer open to UK residents only. **Photocopies not accepted.**